"Noah—"

He eased forward slowly, giving her ample time to stop him. "I can't pretend you don't stir something in me, Callie. And I sure as hell can't pass up this opportunity."

Her mouth felt soft beneath his as he caressed her uninjured cheek. Keeping his touch light, he coaxed her mouth open and slid his tongue in to meet hers.

Callie pulled back and brought her hand to her lips. "Noah, we can't do that."

"Pretty sure we can and did."

"You don't need this complication on top of caring for me, and I can't afford to be sidetracked by you and your charms...and those kisses."

He couldn't help but grin. Apparently he'd found just the thing to distract her.

Dear Reader,

When I started writing my Hollywood series, I knew somewhere along the way I would be introduced to a hunky plastic surgeon. I had no idea he'd be so emotionally damaged, tender and in need of someone to fill the void in his life. Fortunately for this hunky doctor, Callie—in all her feisty, free-spirited ways—enters his life just when he needs her most.

Callie and Noah have goals, dreams and a very different outlook on life. But when one tragedy forces both of them to turn to each other for those dreams to come true, fate steps in and deals them one thing they hadn't been expecting…love.

A plastic surgeon in L.A. is as common as air, but I wanted to give Noah a story that was special. And Callie deserves every dream she's ever wished for because she's fought hard to overcome her own demons. There's nothing like love to heal broken hearts and scarred pasts.

Their romance was such a joy to write and I hope you all love it as much as I did. The way Noah and Callie discover their own beauty within makes this love story really touching. This is one plastic surgeon who learns there's so much more than what's on the surface.

Please drop me a line via my site, www.julesbennett.com, if you enjoyed *Hollywood House Call*. I love hearing from readers!

Cheers!

Jules

JULES BENNETT

HOLLYWOOD HOUSE CALL

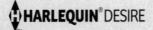

Recycling programs
for this product may
not exist in your area.

ISBN-13: 978-0-373-73250-0

HOLLYWOOD HOUSE CALL

Printed in U.S.A.

www.Harlequin.com

Books by Jules Bennett

Harlequin Desire

Her Innocence, His Conquest #2081
Caught in the Spotlight #2148
Whatever the Price #2181
Behind Palace Doors #2219
Hollywood House Call #2237

Silhouette Desire

Seducing the Enemy's Daughter #2004
For Business...or Marriage? #2010
From Boardroom to Wedding Bed? #2046

Other titles by this author available in ebook format.

JULES BENNETT

National bestselling author Jules Bennett's love of storytelling started when she would get in trouble as a child and would tell her parents her imaginary friends were to blame. Since then, her vivid imagination has taken her down a path she'd only dreamed of. And after twelve years of owning and working in salons, she hung up her shears to write full-time.

Jules doesn't just write Happily Ever After, she lives it. Married to her high school sweetheart, Jules and her hubby have two little girls who keep them smiling. She loves to hear from readers! Contact her at authorjules@gmail.com, visit her website, www.julesbennett.com, where you can sign up for her newsletter, or send her a letter at P.O. Box 396, Minford, OH 45653. You can also follow her on Twitter and join her Facebook fan page.

For my husband, who thinks I'm beautiful
whether I'm wearing a formal dress, jeans and boots
or lounge pants. I love you with all my heart.
Thank you for showing me the beauty of love.

One

"**I** want your body."

Callie Matthews jerked around to see her boss, her very sexy Hollywood-plastic-surgeon boss standing only a few feet away in the foyer of his office. When he reached behind his back, the lock to the front door slid into place with a quick flick of his wrist.

"Excuse me?" she asked, thankful the office was now closed.

A naughty grin spread across Noah Foster's face, showcasing that killer smile that never failed to make women weak in the knees as their panties were dropping. Granted, her panties had always remained in place, but still...

Mercy, she was so shallow, because if he so much as crooked a finger for her to follow him into the break room and...

"Hear me out," he said, holding his hands up. "I know you want to catch your big break by acting—"

O-kay. So they obviously weren't having the same thoughts about him wanting to tear off her underwear in the break room. Such a shame.

"But," he went on, oblivious to her naughty thoughts, "I have a proposition for you."

Those last three words were like music to her ears. That break-room fantasy might come true after all.

"I have an upcoming ad campaign I'd like you to model for."

She shook her head. "I'm sorry. What?"

Model? The chubby teen that still lived inside her nearly laughed. But Callie had long since left that girl behind in Kansas.

Noah moved toward her, never taking his gaze from hers, never breaking that signature smile. "I'd like you to do the modeling for the ad to launch my new office across town."

Callie came to her feet and moved around the desk. "Obviously, you haven't thought this through."

He raked his eyes down her body, sending all kinds of yummy thoughts swirling through her overactive imagination. "Oh, but I have. And it's you I want."

Oh, baby. If only those words were used under different circumstances.

"You have tons of clients you could use," she told him as she turned and marched down the hall to the lounge to retrieve her purse. "Besides, I've never modeled."

Like most transplants to L.A., Callie had come eager to be the next actress that would make Hollywood directors and producers sit up in their chairs and take notice of her remarkable talents. Unfortunately, her agent couldn't get her any auditions that weren't embarrassing. So far she'd done a commercial for zit cream and one for STD meds. Yeah, not the claim to fame she'd been hoping for. But she had to start somewhere, right?

Wait, maybe that whole STD thing was why Noah wasn't so interested in seeing her outside the office. He did know that was purely acting…didn't he? She was free and clear in that department, especially considering her lack of sexual experience. Not that she was a virgin, but she might as well be for the two pathetic encounters she'd had.

"I just want a few pictures of you, Callie." Noah followed her and rested an impressive broad shoulder against the door-jamb. "The ads we're going for will showcase the natural side of surgery, how to stay young and fresh."

Callie mimicked his action and crossed her own arms over her chest and leaned against the counter. "But other than that minor chin scar you did microdermabrasion on, I haven't had anything else done. Isn't that false advertising?"

"Not at all," he argued. "If you had never been a client, then that would be false advertisement. But you're perfect, Callie. You're beautiful, the camera will love you, and you'll be on billboards across town. Tell me you don't want that kind of exposure."

Well, this *was* a giant step up from zit cream and STDs.

"You think this will help with my acting?" she asked.

He shrugged. "It can't hurt."

There was a role coming up in an Anthony Price film that she would give anything for, and her agent had yet to get her an audition. But maybe if she had the right connections…

"I have a proposition to throw back at you," she countered.

Dark brows drew together as his eyes narrowed. "You make me nervous when you get that look. Last time you had a lightbulb moment we ended up with a cappuccino machine in the break room that shot mystery liquid all over the walls and the floor."

She waved a hand through the air. "Minor technical difficulty."

He sighed. "Let's hear it, Callie."

"You talk to Olivia Dane about getting me an audition for this upcoming film of Anthony's and I'll pose for you."

If Noah called the Grande Dane of Hollywood, who just so happened to be their number-one client and mother to the hotshot producer on the new film Callie was aching to get a part in, Callie would forever be grateful.

"I'm not asking you to have her give me a part," she went on when he was silent. "I just want an audition to show them what I can do."

God, she hated to sound as if she was begging, but, well… she was. She'd come to L.A. to pursue a dream, not to get this close and have a door slammed in her face.

Callie believed in fate and it was no coincidence she worked for the same plastic surgeon who catered to all of the needs of the most recognized woman in Hollywood.

"Please," she said, offering a sweet smile.

His brows tipped down as he tilted his head. Damn, he had that George Clooney sultry look down pat.

"Your agent can't get you an audition?" he asked.

Callie shrugged. "She claims this isn't the right role for me. But I can't prove myself if I don't get the chance."

He reached out, placed those large, masculine hands on her shoulders and all sorts of happy tingles spread through her. Mercy, she wanted those hands on her without the barrier of clothing.

One dream at a time, Callie.

"Your agent has been in this business for a while," he told her, his voice softening as if he were trying to explain something to a toddler. "Maybe she knows what she's talking about."

"I don't see how it would hurt," she insisted. "If I don't get it, I'm no worse off. But there's that chance I could land this and launch into something I've been dreaming of my entire life."

Dark gray eyes searched her face. "I can't call her. I know how bad you want this, but I couldn't live with myself if I threw you into a lifestyle that isn't as glamorous as you think it is. You haven't been in town that long, Callie. Why don't you ease into this? Anthony Price is a big deal."

No matter how sexy Noah was, she refused to let him ruin her dream. "Fine. I'll get this audition my own way."

He dropped his hands and placed them on his narrow hips. "Let your agent do the grunt work, Callie. Stars weren't born overnight.

"You're a beautiful woman. You won't have a problem getting attention."

Something very warm spread through her at his declaration. To think a man like Noah Foster thought she was beautiful, a man who created beauty for a living, was one of those compliments she'd keep locked away in her heart forever.

"I'll give you fifty thousand dollars to pose."

Callie froze at his abrupt offer. "Fifty thousand? Are you out of your ever-lovin' mind?"

He chuckled. "You know, when you're shocked, your accent becomes really strong."

"I don't have an accent," she told him. "And get back to that offer. Are you kidding me?"

His smile faded. "I don't kid about business or money."

Fifty thousand could go so far. Her parents needed a new roof desperately and she could buy them a second car, something reliable. God, how could she turn down this offer?

As she ran through the pros and cons—and there were definitely more pros—Noah's eyes studied her in that way that always made her nervous. For one thing, he was a Hollywood surgeon to the stars and she always felt as if he was analyzing her. Another reason was because, well, she found her boss drop-dead, curl-your-toes-into-the-carpet sexy. Why on earth the man was still single was beyond her.

Maybe he slobbered when he kissed—that was a total turn-off. Or maybe he was terrible between the sheets.

As she studied him, she knew there was no way a man like Noah Foster would be a slacker in the sack. The man exuded sex appeal, and he looked so amazingly perfect with clothes on she couldn't even imagine what he did to a birthday suit.

Noah offered that killer, dimpled smile as if to reassure her of her future. He was not fighting fair with those damn twin dimples, and she had a feeling her resolve was going to crumble about as fast as her panties would drop if he'd offer that break-room fantasy of hers.

Yeah, she knew she couldn't turn down that money. As much as she'd wanted him to talk to Olivia, she was grateful for the fact he had so much confidence in her to offer such a large amount.

"I'll do the ad," she told him. "If you're sure my look is what you want plastered on billboards."

Crazy thought, but whatever he wanted. He was the one paying.

"You're exactly the look, Callie. I want to capture that youthfulness, that innocence."

Callie laughed. "I'm not that innocent."

"You moved here less than a year ago and you grew up in the Midwest." His lids lowered slightly over those dark eyes as he leaned forward just enough to get into her personal space. "You're practically still a virgin."

Callie's mouth went dry because the word *virgin* instantly brought to mind sex, and the word *sex* hovered in her mind while Noah stood this close with his bedroom eyes locked onto hers.

"I assure you, I'm not a virgin."

Shut up, Callie.

"Good to know," he told her with that cocky grin. "But I'm glad you've given in to the pictures."

"Have you ever had to fight for anything you want or do you just flash that smile?" she joked.

Something dark passed over his face; his smile faltered, and he swallowed. But just as quick as it came, it passed. "You'd be surprised by what I've had to fight for and what I've lost."

None of her business, she told herself. Everybody had a past, and just because he was a rich, powerful surgeon didn't mean he'd had it easy. But this was the first glimpse she'd had of any kind of pain hidden behind that billion-dollar smile.

She wasn't a virgin.

Noah inwardly groaned. Callie Matthews might not be a virgin in the sexual sense, but she was certainly very innocent because if she had any clue where his thoughts traveled when he thought of her, she'd be suing him for sexual harassment.

He refused to be so clichéd as to date his receptionist, but damn if he didn't want to see her on more personal, intimate terms. He'd played with fire when he'd cornered her two days ago in the lounge. When he'd moved in closer to her, he'd noticed her bright green eyes widening, the way she kept nervously licking her lips…those sexy, naturally full lips that begged to be kissed. His female clients paid a small fortune for a mouth like Callie's.

Noah eased back in his office chair. She'd be coming in any moment and he intended to keep their relationship professional. No more touching, no more getting pulled under by her hopeful eyes and childlike dreams.

If Callie had any idea what she was in for in this Hollywood wannabe-actress cycle, she'd run back to that cornfield she came from. It wasn't all glitz and glamour. There was no way in hell he'd see another woman he cared about fall to the dark side of Hollywood.

The scars from his fiancée were still too fresh, too deep.

And between the house they'd shared that he had to go home to every day and her ailing grandmother he cared for, Noah had a sickening feeling those wounds would never heal.

And Callie reminded him so much of Malinda sometimes it hurt to even think of the bright way his fiancée used to light up over her future career. Callie was Malinda all over again… only this time he refused to get attached.

He raked a hand through his hair, trying to rid himself of the nightmare that still plagued him.

His fiancée had meant everything to him. He'd have done anything in his power to save her. But he'd failed. He'd failed the one woman he'd loved with his whole heart, the one woman he'd wanted to spend the rest of his life with. Noah refused to ever let his heart become entangled again. He honestly didn't think he could afford another crushing loss.

So there was no way he could talk to Olivia about this role for Callie. He was actually using the modeling as a way to keep her from slipping into a darker world that Callie had no clue about. If he could keep her satisfied with the money, the attention from modeling, perhaps she'd reach those stars in her eyes. Maybe she'd let go of this movie-star fetish.

He had to intervene and do something. And no, he didn't care that he was being devious. He couldn't stand by and watch another innocent woman fall victim to the ugly side of the industry.

Because he already had a nugget of worry where his beautiful, naive receptionist was concerned. He knew what he paid her, but he also knew she was always scraping by. Those few commercials she'd done surely hadn't sucked her into the dark world he wanted to keep her from…had they?

Cynicism had never been part of his life until he'd lived with an addict, and he hated that negative vibe that always seemed to spread through him.

The back door to the office opened and shut. He heard

heels click down the tiled hallway, then slow at his office. Noah smiled at the vision that stopped just outside his door.

"Everything okay?" Callie asked, clutching her purse to her shoulder and her lunch bag with the other hand.

"Of course. Why wouldn't it be?"

She gave him a sideways look and a half grin. "Because you're never in the office before me."

That vibrant blue dress hugged her body in a professional yet sexy way, and Noah had to force himself to keep on track and not think about what it would be like to peel that garment down her body...or to think of how she managed to fit anything beneath it. She either had on a thong or nothing. If she was going commando... God, he couldn't go there.

"I had some things to do before my first client showed," he told her, trying to stay professional. "There's a little boy who was recently scarred due to a house fire and might be referred to me. I actually just hung up with a colleague about some options for this boy."

"I remember that referral." Callie smiled wider. "That's what makes you an awesome doctor. I was so excited when you agreed to take on his case."

Noah didn't want her to look at him like some type of savior. And he sure as hell didn't want to get emotionally involved with a child. Children were vulnerable creatures by nature and he worried that his heart simply couldn't take that level of commitment again.

"The boy's aunt is a good client and she asked if I'd look at him. That doesn't mean I can make him perfect. I just have to wait a few weeks because his wounds are still fairly fresh."

"You're at least giving him a chance and hope," Callie told him, still smiling and still looking at him as if he was more than just a doctor. "That in itself is so much, Noah. Don't downplay your talents."

"I'm not, but I'm going into this realistically. There may be nothing I can do, but I'll do everything in my power to help."

Most doctors had a God complex; Noah liked to think he was not one of them. He knew his abilities, his limitations. But he never backed away from a challenge, and he certainly wasn't about to turn away a ten-year-old boy, no matter if the aunt was a client or not. Noah would try to help a burned child regardless of who called.

"You're quiet," he told her. "That means you're thinking. Should I be nervous?"

A wide, vibrant smile spread across her face. "Well, I have news since we talked the other day about the audition."

Oh, no. That smile could only mean one thing....

"I got a call!" she shouted. She stepped farther into his office and dumped her items in the chair across from his desk. "Isn't that awesome? My agent called me when I was on my way home yesterday and said she was able to get me an audition for this Monday."

A dreaded sense of déjà vu spread through him.

"I'm happy for you," he lied. "Make sure you call Marie to see if she can fill in for you."

"I will." She smiled, then looked down, brought her hands up to her face...and burst into tears.

What the hell?

"Callie?"

He moved around his desk to get closer to her. What had just happened? One second she was beaming with joy and the next she was sobbing into her hands.

"Callie?" he repeated softly. "You okay?"

She swiped her damp cheeks and shook her head. "I'm so sorry, Noah. It's just..."

Those moist eyes turned to him, and even with the smudge of mascara, she was still amazingly stunning.

"You wouldn't understand," she told him.

Wouldn't understand? Understand what?

"I've wanted a break and this is it," she told him through a hiccup. "Once I called Olivia—"

"Wait." He held up a hand. "You called Olivia?"

Callie sniffed and nodded. "Yesterday morning. I was calling to remind her of her Botox appointment next week. I just had to take a chance and ask her about an audition. The worst she could've said was no."

Un-freakin'-believable. This was not happening.

"She was impressed with my initiative and said she'd see what she could do." Callie smiled through the tear tracks. "And my agent called last night, so it's a done deal."

He truly didn't think she knew what she was asking for. In Callie's starstruck mind, she probably had this image of Hollywood as all about red carpets and cocktail parties.

But right now she looked so happy how could he not act supportive? She had no family nearby and she'd only talked about her neighbor a handful of times, so he didn't even think she had too many friends. He'd be a total jerk if he didn't at least show some support. Damn the gentleman-like qualities his mother instilled in him.

"I can't believe you used a patient contact," he said. "Don't you think that was overstepping a bit?"

Callie shrugged, but her smile remained. "No. I've become friendly with Ms. Dane. I don't think I abused my power, and I can honestly say I'd do it again, Noah."

He studied her and knew she was fighting for a dream she believed she deserved. He could forgive her anything when she smiled at him that way.

"That's great, Callie." He even gave her his own smile to show her he was happy, then pointed toward her face. "You may want to touch up your makeup before the patients arrive."

Callie gasped, reaching up to pat beneath her eyes. "Oh,

no," she cried when she glanced at her black fingertips. "I'm sure I look like a mess."

"There's nothing you could do that could diminish your beauty."

Without thinking, he reached out to wipe away the tear tracks on her porcelain cheek. As the pad of his thumb slid across her skin, her breath hitched, her eyes held his. How had they gotten this close? Had he stepped toward her or had she come to him?

Her damp eyes dipped down to his lips, then back up.

What he wouldn't give to pull her against him and taste those full lips. Just once. Would that hurt anything?

Oh, yeah. Their working relationship.

"I better go clean up," she told him, backing away and gathering her things from the armchair beside him. As she turned to walk away, she glanced back over her shoulder. "Thank you, Noah. It means a lot to have someone cheering me on."

And now he was a damn hypocrite. But what should he have done when she'd been all teary and smiling? Shot down her dreams right in her face? Showing support and being supportive were two different things…weren't they?

And what the hell had he been thinking? Touching her, complimenting her and getting into her personal space so that he could see the dark green rim around her irises and become spellbound by her fresh, floral scent that always seemed to hover around the office.

She'd already been looking at him as if he was some saint. He didn't want that. He wanted Callie, but not on a deeper level than the physical. Anything else would be insane. But his hormones weren't getting that message.

Damn it, he had to gain some control. Beautiful women were his bread and butter, but there was something so innocent, so vibrant about Callie that he found intriguing. She wasn't jaded or bitter like most women he knew. And perhaps that was why he found her so fascinating and why he wanted to keep her that way.

Now, if he could just remember that professional relationship they had, maybe he could stop imagining her naked and wrapped around him.

He couldn't get too close to Callie. He'd sworn to never get involved with anyone again. Besides, she worked for him. Wasn't that reason enough to keep his distance?

Damn if he didn't want to seduce her. He'd never experienced such a strong sexual pull with a woman. And all the signs were there that she was just as attracted.

But he had to keep his distance. There were too many similarities between Malinda and Callie. The stubbornness, the stars in their eyes, the naive way they went after their goals. Not to mention that fiery-red hair and that porcelain skin. Noah couldn't let his heart get mixed up or broken again. But he also couldn't stand by and watch Callie ruin her life.

He'd stick close to her to make sure she didn't make any life-altering decisions that could destroy her.

God help him for the torture he was about to endure by making Callie Matthews his top priority.

Two

Callie's hands were literally shaking. Was this really happening? Was the door of opportunity finally opening for her? Granted she'd been in L.A. a little less than a year and most people took much longer, if ever, to get the audition that would launch their careers.

But Callie had not only gotten the audition nearly two weeks ago, she'd completely nailed it. And her agent had just called to inform her she'd landed the part. It wasn't huge, but she had lines and three scenes with the lead actors. Now she just had to prove herself, make that role shine and wait for other opportunities to come her way.

She squeezed her steering wheel and let out a squeal as she drove toward Noah's office. She couldn't get there fast enough to tell him the good news. Today was her half day to work, so Marie would be there, too, to share in her good news.

This was it. She was finally going to put the old Callie to rest and have everything she'd ever wanted. She'd landed the part; next she would pose for some pictures for Noah and get the money to help her parents in a major way. God, they'd be so happy for a little more security in their lives, and she couldn't wait to be the one to give it to them.

Her whole life she'd been overshadowed by her siblings—her übersmart brother, who was about to graduate college after attending on a full academic scholarship, and her homecoming-queen sister. Callie had been the average middle child. Because she hadn't excelled at sports, academics or popularity, she was most often forgotten. Well, no more being overlooked…by anybody.

Callie knew she looked like a complete moron driving down the road with a wide grin on her face, but she didn't care. For an overweight girl who'd come out of Kansas with big dreams, she'd finally gotten the break of a lifetime.

All her college years of hard work, dieting and exercising before coming to L.A. had paid off. Her goal of becoming an actress was within her reach. That chubby teen in her mind could just shut up because that naive girl with low self-esteem didn't exist anymore.

Callie shoved aside the humiliating years of her past and focused on the happiness she felt now. No way would she let those old insecurities and her school days of being bullied and made fun of come into play. This was her moment to remember, her moment to shine in the glorious fact that she was going to be in the next Anthony Price movie.

Callie pulled up close to the office and barely got her old Honda in park before she was out and racing across the parking lot. Thankfully it was almost lunchtime and the last of the clients should be finishing up before the office was closed for an hour break.

When she entered the cool, air-conditioned building, Marie, the fill-in receptionist, greeted her.

"Hey, Callie," the elderly woman greeted, a smile beaming across her surgically smooth face. "Someone looks very happy today."

Callie couldn't hide her excitement. "I got the part," she all but yelled. "I can't believe it. I got it."

Marie jumped up from her chair, came around the desk and threw her arms around Callie.

"I'm so excited for you," Marie said as she squeezed her.

"You may not be excited when I have to quit once filming starts." Callie eased back. "You'll be swamped with extra hours."

Marie laughed. "I'll make sure he hires someone else, though no one could replace you."

The compliment warmed Callie. "Is Noah wrapping up back there?"

Marie nodded. "Mrs. McDowell is getting her stitches out and then he'll be all done. Go on back to his office, and I'll make sure he knows you're here."

"Don't tell him the news." Callie shifted her bag higher on her shoulder. "I want it to be a surprise. Actually, don't even tell him I'm here. You can just let him know someone is in his office."

Marie giggled. "I like how you think. I'll make sure he goes straight there."

Callie turned to the right, toward Noah's office and away from the patient rooms. She couldn't wait to tell him, to share her excitement and accomplishment.

She went in and took a seat behind his desk in the big, oversize leather chair. Maybe it was not professional to get cozy at his desk, but she honestly didn't think he'd mind. Easing her bag to the floor beside her, she crossed her legs and waited.

She'd tried to call her parents on her way here, but the phone had been disconnected…again. She couldn't get that fifty thousand fast enough. She'd buy the new roof, a reliable new car and prepay some of their utilities for a few months.

With her father still laid off from the chemical plant and his unemployment long since run out, Callie's mother was pulling double shifts at the local grocery store to make ends meet…and they weren't meeting very well.

Guilt ate at Callie. How could she spend all the money she made on herself when her parents were facing such desperate times? She knew families all across the country were struggling, but it was hard to see the ones she loved fall on hard times.

Besides, she'd do something for herself with the money she made from the movie. God knew she could use a new car, as well. Her poor Honda needed to be laid to rest years ago. She couldn't wait to go car shopping. To find something that really said *I've arrived*.

Before her thoughts turned too shallow and she could imagine the color of the car she'd look best in, Noah stood in his doorway. She didn't give him an opportunity to speak before she jumped from the chair and screamed, "I got the part!"

Noah froze for a moment as if to process her words, then he crossed the room and she suddenly found herself coming out from behind the desk, meeting him halfway and being enveloped in a strong, masculine hold.

Oh. My. God.

Had she known he felt this good, this…hard all over, she would've insisted on good-morning hugs every day he came into the office—a much better pick-me-up than coffee. When you could feel a man's rippled muscles beneath his clothing, you knew there was some mighty fine workmanship beneath that cotton.

Noah eased back, keeping a firm grip on her bare biceps. "You seem really happy."

"I've never been happier," she told him, the thrill of her phone call still running through her.

"Then I'm excited for you," he said, letting his hands fall away.

"I feel like celebrating."

He laughed. "Don't celebrate too much and forget the photo shoot in the morning."

Callie smiled. "I know when it is. I'll be there."

Noah studied her face, and Callie refused to look away. When a man like Noah Foster held your gaze, you didn't want to focus your attention on anything else.

"What do you say to dinner to celebrate?" he asked suddenly.

"Dinner?"

Noah's rich laughter washed over her…and she was still tingling from his touch. "Callie, I understand what it's like not to have your family here. Someone needs to share this time with you."

Callie recalled him saying some time back that his family lived in Northern California. Other than that, the topic had been off the table, so she'd assumed that meant for her not to ask any questions about them. But that didn't stop the questions from whirling around in her mind.

"When should we go?" Callie asked, knowing there was no way she would turn down personal time with Noah.

"How about after work?" he suggested, sliding out of his white lab jacket and hanging it on the back of his office door. "Our afternoon is light. We may even get out early."

Callie glanced down at her clothes. While she might look fine, she'd want to freshen up.

"You could leave your car here," he continued. "I'll drive."

Callie wasn't going to turn that offer down. This might not be a date, but it was as close as she would get to dating her hunky boss—though she wasn't under any delusions that Noah would fall for her type. Though so far, from what she could tell, he didn't have any particular type. So why hadn't he ever asked her out?

Oh, yeah. She worked for him.

So what? This was L.A. Did a code of ethics really matter in a land full of sin and silicone? Either something else held him back or he simply wasn't attracted to her. Either way, she had her work cut out for her if she wanted to pursue anything beyond a professional relationship with him. Granted, she had her sights set on her career, but she could so carve some time out of her day for scenery like Noah Foster. And she knew he wasn't a long-term type of guy, so really, what could the harm be in getting to know each other on a personal level?

"Where will we go?" she asked, following him out of his office and down the hall toward the break room.

He threw a killer smile over his shoulder. "You pick. It's your night, Callie."

She mulled it over, thinking of where she'd always wanted to go but never could justify going alone or paying such high prices. This milestone really deserved to be done up right.

Then she remembered the one place she'd always wanted to go but never got a chance.

She offered a wide grin. "Oh, I have the perfect place in mind."

Of all the restaurants Callie could've picked in L.A., Noah couldn't believe she'd chosen this one. A pizza place with games that spit out tickets so you could pick out prizes at the end. On a Friday night this place was crazy with kids running amok, screaming, laughing and waving their generic prizes in the air.

And Callie seemed to be fitting right in.

This was not what he'd envisioned when he'd told her to choose a place. But she'd laughed as she'd smacked the mole heads that kept popping up through holes, and she'd been a major sharpshooter at the "shooting range." Now she was off to a driving game while he stood fisting a wad of bright yellow tickets.

Bright yellow. If Callie Matthews was a color, she'd be yellow. The woman was always happy, always bubbly and never failed to take him by surprise.

And he hadn't necessarily lied when he'd told her he was happy for her. Seeing her beaming from ear to ear had stirred something in him. While he still wasn't thrilled at the possibility of her innocence being shattered, he couldn't let her celebrate alone.

Her sweet naïveté was getting to him. And she had no idea the power she was holding over him.

His cell vibrated in his pocket and he slid it out, smiling when he saw the number.

"So you are alive," he said in place of a traditional hello.

"Kiss ass."

Noah laughed at his best friend and Hollywood heartthrob, Max Ford. "When a whole week goes by and I know you're not filming, I have to assume you're either dead or getting some serious action. Glad to know you're still with us."

"Oh, I'm alive," Max assured him. "Where are you? It sounds like you're at a kid's birthday party."

Noah glanced around the open room where kids ran from game to game, parents chasing to keep up with the chaos. His gaze circled back to Callie and he watched her steering intensely at the racing game.

"You wouldn't believe me if I told you."

"You're moonlighting as a clown for kids' parties, aren't you?" Max joked. "I'm not sure the ladies will go for the Bozo wig, pal."

Noah laughed. "Did you call to annoy me or do you have a point?"

"I wanted to know if you were free tomorrow. Haven't seen you for a while. Thought we could get together."

Callie jumped from her racing chair and grinned like a kid as the machine spit out another row of bright yellow tickets. Her enthusiasm was contagious, and he found himself standing in the middle of the room with a silly grin on his face. When was the last time he truly grinned because he wanted to and not because he felt forced to please his current company?

"Actually, tomorrow is the photo shoot for the ads for my new office," Noah told him. "But I should be free in the evening if all goes as planned."

"I thought you were still looking for a model."

When Callie turned and caught his eye, he motioned that he was stepping outside. She nodded and moved on to another game.

"Callie is doing it for me," Noah said, walking toward the door to move farther away from the noise.

"Callie Matthews? Damn, she's hot. How did you manage that? Has she done modeling before?"

Once outside, Noah took a seat on the bench next to the door. "No, but I'm trying to watch out for her. She's got stars in her eyes, man. And she just got a pretty good-size role in a new Anthony Price film."

"Noah, you can't save everybody," Max told him with a sigh. "You've got to let go of the past."

"Easier said than done."

"Had any more offers on the house?" Max asked.

"Just the two."

"Which you turned down?"

Noah rubbed a hand over his head and glanced through the door to see Callie smiling while tackling another game. "Yes. I turned them down."

"And you're still going to see Thelma every day?"

Noah's chest tightened. "I'm all she has."

"She's not even your family, Noah. You have to let go. I understand she's Malinda's grandmother, but you've been paying her assisted-living bills for a year now. She has Alzheimer's. She won't know if you don't show up. You've got to bury the past."

He sighed. "I'll bury it when it's time."

"Good," his friend said. "You can start by asking Callie out on a date. She'd be perfect."

"I'm not asking her out," Noah replied. At least, he wouldn't ask her on a *real* date.

"Great. Then you won't mind if—"

"Yes, I would mind." Noah cut him off. "You've got enough on your plate without adding Callie to the mix."

Max's laughter nearly vibrated Noah's phone. "You can't keep dibs on her and not do anything about it. You're both adults. If you want to go beyond business and get personal, what's stopping you?"

"She's the best receptionist I've ever had. I'd like to keep her for a while."

"She'll probably be leaving when she starts acting, anyway, so why not just go for it now instead of torturing yourself?" Max asked. "You know you've thought about it."

Thought about it, fantasized about it. Had taken the proverbial cold showers to prove it.

Noah came to his feet, glancing inside at Callie, who was looking toward the doors, probably looking for him.

"Listen, I need to go," Noah said. "I'll call you tomorrow and let you know what time I'll be free."

After sliding the phone into his pocket, he went back inside. Callie's smile across the crowded room did something funny to his chest…something he'd rather not explore.

"I'm ready to cash in my winnings," she told him, holding up her tickets. "I've got a hundred here and I think I gave you a hundred. Let's go see what I can get."

Noah followed her as he pulled her tickets from his pocket. He still couldn't believe this was her idea of celebrating. She certainly wasn't like all the other women he knew. Their idea of celebrating would be to head to the most expensive restaurant and try to get into his bed afterward...not that he ever complained about those nights.

But Callie was different—a fact he'd known from the first day of working with her. She was like a breath of fresh air. He never knew what to expect from her, but he knew it would be something great.

After she chose her prizes—a hideous monkey with tie-dyed fur and a flower-shaped eraser—he escorted her to the car and drove back to his office. Even though she was fairly silent during the ride, she was beaming from ear to ear.

"You had a good time."

It wasn't a question, more like an observation.

"A blast," she told him. "I'd always wanted to go to a place like that as a kid."

He threw her a glance as he pulled up beside her car. "Why didn't you?"

Callie's smile faltered, and she toyed with the ear on the monkey. "I didn't have a very pleasant childhood. And that's the best way I can put it."

Noah put the car in Park and turned to face her. "I'm sorry, Callie. I didn't mean to pry. You've worked for me for a while now and I don't know much about your life before you came here."

She attempted a smile, but her sad gaze met his. "I'd rather focus on my life here than back home."

Wherever she came from, whatever she experienced must be painful because the L.A. Callie was a bright, bubbly woman who didn't care to let everyone see how positive she was about life.

"I can't thank you enough for everything, Noah." She

reached out, placed a hand on his forearm. "You don't know how much I value our friendship. At least, I like to think we're friends."

"We are," he said, cursing his voice when it cracked like some damn adolescent.

Her dainty, warm hand on his arm really shouldn't turn him on, but he'd been intrigued by her for a while now.

"Good," she said, smiling wider. "It's nice to know I have people I can count on."

She leaned over and gave him an innocent, simple peck on his cheek, but as she pulled back, her face remained within a breath of his and she locked eyes with him again. He froze and was surprised when she placed a softer kiss on his lips, hesitating as if waiting for approval.

"I'm sorry," she whispered. "Was that unprofessional?"

"Not as much as this."

He cupped the side of her face and claimed her lips.

Three

Callie knew on some level this was wrong—that would be the professional level.

But on a personal, feminine level, kissing Noah Foster was so, *so* perfectly right. There was no way she could not respond to such a blatant advance.

His thumbs trailed along her jawline as he shifted and changed the angle. Mercy, this man could kiss her lips and she felt it all the way down to her toes…not to mention all the important spots in between.

Callie grabbed hold of his biceps as the glorious assault on her mouth continued. This attraction wasn't new on his side or he wouldn't be devouring her mouth in such a way that had her limbs trembling and her thighs clenching.

But before she could bask in the fact this was the best kiss she'd ever experienced, Noah pulled back.

"God, Callie," he all but growled. "I'm—"

"No." She shook her head, putting a bit of distance between them so she could look in his eyes. "Don't say you're sorry."

His eyes searched hers, that warm gaze dropping to her lips before coming back up. "I wasn't. I was going to say I don't know what came over me, but that would be a lie. I've wanted to do that for some time."

The revelation wasn't surprising, but she was a little taken aback that he admitted it. Which brought to mind the all-important question: Why hadn't they locked lips before now? Had she known he had such…talents, she would've taken charge months ago.

Okay, well, maybe she would've held back since he was her boss, but she definitely would've fantasized about it more.

"So have I," she admitted.

The corners of Noah's sexy, and she could now add tasty, mouth lifted. "But you work for me."

"So now what?" she asked. God, that sounded lame. "I mean, I don't have to quit, do I?"

"Do you want to quit?"

Callie quirked a brow. "Don't answer my question with a question."

"Just trying to figure my way around this…."

She grinned. "By this, you mean the fact that I want you?"

He studied her face. "Yes."

Callie's hands slipped from his thick arms. "I won't lie about my feelings, Noah. If that makes you uncomfortable…"

"I'm not uncomfortable," he told her. "I won't deny the sexual tension between us."

The chubby girl who still lived deep inside her couldn't believe this was happening. The new Callie, the one who took charge of her life and made things happen, knew this was a moment she'd remember forever.

Noah Foster, one of the sexiest men she'd ever met, was admitting he was sexually attracted to her.

"I don't do relationships, but I can't deny the chemistry is strong here. I've never been in this situation before, and I'm trying to keep this simple."

Intrigued, and a little surprised that he inadvertently admitted that she had the upper hand here, Callie grinned.

"And what situation is that?" she asked. "Making out in your car with an employee?"

With a sigh, Noah turned in his seat, laughed and shook his head. "You're not going to make this easy, are you?"

"What's that?"

Throwing her a glance and a wicked sideways smile, he said, "Oh, now you're going to answer a question with a question."

"Touché."

"How about we go on a date and see where this leads?" he asked. "Since the attraction is mutual, I don't see why we couldn't."

Callie's belly quivered. She had no doubt that if they went out they'd probably continue where they left off with that kiss. Because a kiss that held those kinds of promises was just a stepping-stone straight to the bedroom. The possibilities thrilled and aroused her, but she also had to be realistic. She didn't want to cause any awkward moments in the office. Though right now she was feeling anything but awkward.

"Tell you what." She shifted sideways and smiled. "When I start filming, I'll go on that date, but not before I quit my job. Deal?"

His eyes roamed over her face, pausing on her lips, then back up to her eyes. "I already told you I can't do a relationship, anyway, so it doesn't matter when to me. I'd rather see you outside the office now, but that's because I'm not a patient man."

She laughed. "Boy, you really lay on the charm, huh?"

He shrugged. "I won't lie. I worry about you getting mixed

up in this Hollywood scene so fast." He blew out a sigh, not wanting to scare her. "I know it's not my place, but…"

"I'll be fine, Noah," she assured him. "This is what I've always dreamed about. There's no need to worry."

He looked out the windshield and off into the distance. "You have no idea," he murmured.

He'd initially worried about exploring his attraction to Callie because he was her boss, but if he kept her close, maybe then he could also keep her safe. He knew he couldn't save everyone. He hadn't been able to save Malinda, but he damn well couldn't watch another woman get hurt if he could prevent her downfall. If he could only save one woman, he wanted it to be Callie.

Callie gathered her things, including that heinous monkey, and tugged at the door handle. "I better get going. Thanks again for everything."

Before she exited the car, she leaned in and kissed him. Not a friendly peck, but a soft, open-lipped kiss right near the corner of his mouth.

Oh, yeah, it was going to be a long, long wait for that film to start shooting next month.

Noah paced, checked his watch and paced back the other way. He not only had to get this shoot over with, he needed to run by the assisted-living facility to check on Thelma. He wasn't happy with the afternoon nurse and he wanted to pop in unannounced. And then he planned to meet up with Max.

"Listen, Noah, I can only give about five more minutes," the photographer told him. "Then I'm going to have to reschedule. I have another shoot later this afternoon I need to set up for."

Hands on his hips, Noah stopped and nodded to the photographer. "I'm sorry, man. I've tried her cell several times.

This isn't like her to be late or blow off a job. She's very professional."

They hadn't been out late the night before, but had she gone back out? Flashes of Malinda making promises to show somewhere flooded his mind. He'd usually found her at home, strung out and totally out of touch with reality.

He hated to think the worst of Callie, but he'd been lied to and deceived for so long before Malinda's death that it was just hard to trust anymore. Added to that, he wondered where Callie put all her money. She always packed her lunch and drove a clankity, beat-up old Honda. He hadn't seen any signs of drug use, but most new users didn't use all the time, and the signs were slow in coming. Besides, just how well did he know Callie aside from at the office? For all he knew, she partied all weekend.

The image of Malinda just before her death, dark eyes, pale skin and sunken cheeks, still haunted him and he'd hate to see the vibrant Callie Matthews fall into that dark abyss.

Callie had always been a professional, though, and she had never been late for anything. She was a bright spirit and he wanted to believe deep in his heart she was an innocent. Something was wrong.

He pulled his cell from his pocket and tried calling again while the photographer started taking down his equipment. A sinking feeling settled deep in his gut each time her chipper voice mail clicked on.

He'd left enough messages and texts, so he hung up and slid the phone back into his pants pocket.

"I'll pay you for your time today, Mark," Noah said. "Can we go ahead and reschedule for next Saturday? Same time?"

Mark nodded. "Sure thing. And don't worry about paying me today. Things happen."

Noah helped Mark carry the lighting and some other equipment to his waiting car. By the time all of that was done and

Mark had left, almost another hour had passed and still there was no word from Callie.

If he weren't so worried, he'd leave her be. She was an adult, after all. But there was a niggling feeling in the back of his mind that something wasn't right. Whether she was hung over or had been in an accident, he didn't know.

Before he stopped at the assisted-living home, Noah thought he should at least drive by Callie's place to check on her. She was, after all, alone in L.A. with no family here and no roommate. He just needed to make sure she was okay.

Endless possibilities flooded his mind. As morbid thought after morbid thought raced through his head, his cell rang. Panic filled him instantly, but relief slithered through. Hopefully that was Callie on the other end ready to apologize for being late.

But when he glanced at the caller ID and saw Private Caller, his hope died. He punched the button on his car to put the call on speaker as he drove down the freeway toward her apartment.

"Hello?"

"Mr. Foster?"

Not recognizing the voice, he answered, "Yes."

"This is Marcia Cooper. I'm a nurse in the E.R. at Cedars-Sinai Medical Center. We have a Miss Matthews, who was brought in to us. We tried calling one of her neighbors, but we couldn't get her. Callie suggested we try you next."

Fear gripped Noah, but if she'd mentioned his name and number she was at least coherent. "Is she all right?"

"I really cannot discuss her condition over the phone," the nurse told him. "Are you able to come in?"

"I'll be right there."

Noah pushed the pedal farther, weaving in and out as best he could with the thick afternoon traffic. The thought of Callie hurting in any way made his stomach clench. He'd only known her to be vivacious, full of life and always smiling.

He understood the nurse was not able to disclose any information due to privacy laws, but knowing Callie was in the E.R. and not knowing her condition scared him more than before he'd gotten the phone call. Did she have a cut that just needed stitches? Had she fallen and hit her head? Had she been attacked?

Damn it. Where had she been when she'd gotten hurt?

A vision of his late fiancée crumpled on their bedroom floor flashed through his mind, but he quickly blocked the image. He couldn't travel down that path. Right now, Callie needed him.

Noah parked in the doctor's lot, thanks to his pass. He had privileges at several L.A. hospitals, including Cedars-Sinai, thank God.

He ran into the entrance and quickly made his way to the Emergency Department.

"Noah."

He turned to see Dr. Rich Bays, an associate he knew quite well, coming toward him.

"You here for a patient?"

"Yeah," Noah said. "Callie Matthews. Are you treating her?"

Rich nodded. "I am. She's in room seven."

"How is she?"

"I'll fill you in as we go to her room." Rich motioned for him to walk with him. "She has a deep facial laceration that extends from her temple down to her mandible and a fractured right clavicle. The CT scan should be back anytime and I'll be in to let her know what it says. From what I'm told of the car accident, she's very lucky things aren't worse."

Deep facial laceration. As a plastic surgeon, he'd seen some severe cases, but he didn't even want to think how serious Callie's case was because whatever was wrong, he would fix it.

"Is she being admitted for observation?" Noah asked.

Rich nodded. "For the night. Even if the scan comes back clear, she was unconscious when she was brought in." Dr. Bays stopped outside the glass sliding door. "And when she goes home, she'll probably need help."

Noah nodded. "I'll make sure she's cared for."

No doubt Callie would brush off the help, but he wasn't letting her go through this alone. Either she'd stay with him or he could stay at her apartment.

Another thought slammed through him. How would this affect the role she'd just landed? Didn't filming start soon?

God, he hadn't wanted her to get the part, but he sure as hell hadn't wanted her injured or scarred. Did she even know the severity of her wound? The broken bone would heal, but the injury to her face...

A deep laceration could take a year to heal, depending on the tissue that was damaged. Possible surgeries filled his mind. No matter how many she needed, he would be the one seeing to all of her medical care.

He needed to assess her injuries before he jumped to any conclusions. She might not be as bad as he was imagining... or she could be worse. That sickening knot in his stomach clenched so tightly he thought he'd be sick.

Noah knew one thing for certain, though. No other plastic surgeon was going to be putting his surgical hands on Callie. He'd do the job and make sure it was done right. Perfection in the O.R. was his life and he'd settle for no less with Callie.

"She's in here." Rich nodded toward the closed door. "I'm going to check to see if that scan is back yet. I'll be back as soon as I learn anything."

"Thanks, Rich."

Noah steeled himself for what he'd see on the other side of

the door and privacy curtain. He told himself that as a doctor he'd seen it all, but the thought of Callie wrapped and damaged scared him on a level he didn't think still existed after he'd faced the hell he'd gone through in the past two years.

He wasn't going to lie, wasn't even going to try to deny the fear that coursed through him and nearly had a choke hold on him.

Too many times he'd seen Malinda at her worst. But he'd never seen Callie as anything but bright, smiling and joyful.

He knew he needed to be strong for Callie so he took a deep breath, eased open the door and stepped in. When he pulled aside the thick curtain, his knees nearly buckled. Her whole face, save for her eyes and mouth, was wrapped in white gauze, her hair puffed out in a matted mess around it. Her arm was in a sling to protect her broken collarbone. She looked so frail, so lifeless lying there.

He had to mentally distance himself from this or he'd never be strong enough to help her. Damn it, he had to be a friend first, not a doctor, not a boss and certainly not a wannabe lover.

As he eased closer to the bed, her eyes shifted to lock onto his.

"Hell of a way to get out of the photo shoot," he said, trying to lighten the moment.

"God, Noah," she whispered. "I'm sorry. So sorry. I was on my way to the shoot and a truck came out of nowhere.... I don't remember anything between seeing a semi and waking up here."

She started to weep and Noah's heart constricted. Other than the happy tears in his office, he'd never seen her cry, had never seen anything from her but smiles and happiness—which was why he'd considered her the color yellow. Cheerful and sweet.

He wondered if she'd seen her face or if Rich had told her how bad the injuries were.

The doctor in Noah wanted to demand to see her chart so he could review it, but she needed to be consoled, needed to know everything would be all right. Because no matter what care she needed, he'd see to it himself. And he didn't mean hire a nurse. He'd literally see to her every need personally. Even if he had to refer his clients for the next few weeks to a colleague, he would do everything in his power to make her comfortable and secure.

"Callie." He moved over to the edge of the bed, taking her good hand in his. "There's absolutely nothing to apologize about. Nothing."

"I'm sorry to have to bother you, but I didn't know who else to call when my neighbor wasn't home," she told him, trying to turn her head away.

"I wouldn't be anywhere else." He squeezed her hand. "What can I do for you?"

She tried to shake her head, wincing at the obvious pain.

"Just try to relax." He stroked the back of her hand with his thumb. "I'm not going anywhere, Callie."

"I'll be fine," she assured him, but her voice cracked as tears filled her eyes again. "I know they're keeping me tonight, but I'll have my neighbor take me home when I get released tomorrow. You don't have to stay."

"I'll leave if you really want me to, but when you're dismissed, I'm taking you home with me."

She slid her hand from his and tried to roll over, only to gasp when she realized she'd rolled onto her bad side.

"Easy, Callie. Don't be so stubborn. You're going to need help, and since I'm a doctor, I think the best place for you is with me."

She didn't respond. Silence filled the room and Noah knew

she didn't want his help. Too bad. He wasn't going to leave her like this.

"Do you want me to try your neighbor again?" he asked. "You can give me the number."

"No," Callie said softly. "I don't need a babysitter. I know I need someone, but…God, Noah, I don't want to be here. I don't *want* to need someone."

Before he could say anything further, Rich stepped into the room and slid back the curtain.

"CT scan looks good," he said. "But I'm going to go ahead and get a room ready for you just for overnight observation. You were unconscious when you were brought in and I'd feel more comfortable monitoring you for a bit. You should be able to go home in the morning. Have you thought about who can help you there?"

"I'll manage," she told him, still keeping her face turned to the far wall.

"Miss Matthews, I can't let you go without knowing you'll be taken care of."

Noah shot Rich a look and whispered, "I'll take her."

Rich merely nodded and left the room.

"I'm not going to stay with you," Callie said. "I'll be fine at home."

"Then I can stay with you," he told her, trying not to get angry over her stubbornness.

"I know I should have someone to help, but I'll call my neighbor or you if I absolutely have to. I want to be alone."

Noah refused to back down. "Well, that's too bad. I'm going to help you, Callie, whether you want it or not. So you can decide right now if you want to be difficult or if you want to cooperate. The end result will be the same."

Slowly, she turned to face him. "End result? And what is the end result, Noah? That I'll never be able to start filming this movie? That my dream was just pulled out from under me? They won't wait on me to heal, if I ever do heal. I'll never be the same."

God, he hadn't wanted her to do the film, but he'd certainly never wished for anything bad to happen to her. And if he hadn't insisted she model for him, she wouldn't be in this damn bed wrapped up and broken.

Sobs tore through the room and Callie pounded the bed with her left fist. "Don't you see, Noah? The end result is that my life and everything I've ever worked for were just taken away."

Noah took her hand once more and laced his fingers with hers. "I'll make this right, Callie. No matter what I have to do, I'll make you whole again."

He hated that he was now torn between his present and his past. He wanted to stay with her, but he had to get to the assisted-living facility.

He left Callie resting, as well as she could, considering, and headed out the door. If he hadn't needed to see the afternoon nurse Thelma had been complaining about, he wouldn't have left Callie's side…no matter what she said.

For all he knew, the afternoon nurse was perfectly fine. After all, Thelma did have Alzheimer's and still believed her granddaughter and he were engaged to be married. Noah had never told her any different. Why upset the poor woman when she wouldn't remember it the next time he went to see her?

As he walked up to the front doors of the facility, he pulled his cell from his pocket and dialed Max. Of course the call went to voice mail because the man was rarely available. One of these days he was going to get really burned-out on work.

"Hey, Max," Noah said after the beep. "I can't make it tonight. Callie was in a pretty bad accident so I'll be with her. Text or call when you get a chance."

He slid the phone back into his pocket and entered the glass double doors. An elderly lady greeted him. It was the same white-haired lady who sat by the door every time he came to visit Thelma. Supposedly, the woman was waiting on her husband to come pick her up, but Noah had been told the lady's husband had passed away over ten years ago.

Alzheimer's was a fickle bitch and it sickened Noah that so many people were affected by it. As always, he smiled to the lady and made his way down the narrow carpeted hallway.

Thelma's room was the last one on the left, and as usual, her door was closed. According to Malinda, she'd never been much of a social butterfly even before the disease. Since Noah never knew Thelma before she got sick, he had only Malinda's opinion to go on.

Noah tried the knob, not surprised to find it locked. Tapping his knuckles against the wood door, he called out. "It's Noah, Thelma."

After a moment, he heard shuffling from inside the room before there was a soft click and the door eased open.

Her short silver hair was matted on one side and in the back—a sure sign she'd been asleep in her recliner again.

"How are you feeling today?" he asked, stepping into the room that inevitably was hotter than Satan's personal sauna. Why did the elderly need their heat on full throttle in the middle of summer?

"A little tired today," she told him, moving across the room to her old green chair positioned in front of the TV. "You caught me in the middle of my soaps."

Noah laughed as he eased behind her to turn the heat down. His shirt was already sticking to his back.

"I won't stay long," he promised as he took a seat on the edge of the bed that faced her. "Did you have lunch?"

She stared at him, those blue eyes full of doubt and confusion. "I believe so. Can't recall what I had. Let's see…ham sandwich? No, that wasn't it. Chicken soup. I think."

Noah nodded like he always did. He knew she wouldn't recall, but he was buying some time until the nurse was due in.

"Where's Malinda today?" Thelma asked, her eyes widening and a smile spreading across her face. "I want to hear all about the wedding details."

This was never an easy topic to broach. Not only because he still felt that emptiness Malinda had left in his life, but because he hated lying to this sweet woman, even if she wouldn't remember the truth. Even with the disease robbing her memory, Thelma knew there was a void in her life.

"She couldn't come today," he said honestly.

"That girl works too hard," Thelma replied as she pulled the handle on her recliner. "You tell her that her grandmother wants to see her. I have some wedding ideas I want to discuss with her."

Noah nodded and smiled as always. Though the smiling was costing him. He hated standing there discussing a wedding that would never be, to a woman who was dead, with someone who wouldn't remember this conversation five minutes later. But Thelma still had hope shining in her eyes and he wasn't about to take away the one thing she held on to.

"I'll be right back, Thelma." He moved to the door and propped it open. "I'm just going to step outside your room to look for someone."

She didn't answer, but her soap opera had come back on and she had that tunnel-vision look as she smiled at the characters on TV.

Noah moved into the hall to look for the nurse. Thelma's pills were supposed to be distributed with her breakfast and lunch and just before bedtime. But a few of her prescriptions hadn't been refilled on time and Thelma had claimed she didn't recall seeing the nurse at lunchtime very often. Thelma's fading mind might be to blame, but he couldn't take the chance that she wasn't getting the best care.

When Noah saw the nurse in question come out of a room down the hall, he hurried to catch up with her.

"Excuse me, Lori."

She turned and smiled. "Yes, Mr. Foster?"

"I was wondering if I could speak to you about Thelma."

The nurse nodded as her eyes darted down the hall toward Thelma's room. "Of course. Is something wrong?"

"Has she had her pills today?" he asked.

"She's had all of the medication she gets on my shift. Why?"

He hated to think this nurse wasn't doing her job, but he would keep a closer eye on the meds and make sure Thelma was getting her daily doses.

"No reason. Just making sure," he said with a smile. "She forgets and tells me she hasn't had any."

Lori nodded and patted his arm. "It's the disease. Robs their minds. I assure you she's being taken care of."

"Thanks. That's good to hear."

She dropped her hand. "If you'll excuse me, I need to see to another resident."

As she scurried off, Noah had that gut feeling that always settled deep within him whenever Malinda would lie to him about where she'd been. He wanted to believe Lori, but he wasn't naive. He would keep his eye on her and make more appearances in the afternoon during lunch breaks. No matter the cost, he couldn't let his late fiancée's grandmother down. He was all she had left.

More than likely Lori was clean, but that cynicism ran deep and he had major issues taking someone's word at face value.

As he went back to spend a few more minutes with Thelma, he checked his watch. He didn't want to be gone from Callie very long. No matter how stubborn she was going to be during this process, he could be more so.

No matter what it took, he'd see Callie through her recovery, and if he had to lock her inside his house to do it, then so be it.

One woman was not only hurt on his watch, she'd died. He'd damn well never let that happen again. No matter how he had to rearrange his life.

And beyond the guilt lay an attraction that he couldn't fight. But what scared him the most was that he didn't know if he even wanted to.

Waves of emotions flooded through Callie as she settled into Noah's luxury SUV. Her body ached all over from the accident yesterday, but the physical pain was nothing compared to the emotional pain of having her dream of becoming an actress destroyed. She'd never act or model for Noah and she'd never get that money to send home.

She'd never be able to play her role in the Anthony Price movie, which would start filming next month. Her face was all bandaged up, but she'd seen the damage beneath. She knew the ugliness that waited for her on the other side of the white gauze. The role of a royal beauty couldn't be played by a woman who looked like an Egyptian mummy.

All those thoughts whirled around in her mind, bumping into each other and exacerbating her nausea, brought on by meds.

"Whatever is going through your head, get it out." Noah brought the engine to life and pulled from the curb of her apartment complex, where they'd stopped to pick up her things on the way to his place. "As a doctor I know the impact positive thinking can have on recuperation. You have to stay focused on the good here, Callie."

She turned her head to look out the window. "Just drive."

"You can talk to me, you know."

Callie fought back tears. The man was relentless. He'd come back to her room yesterday and stayed overnight with her as if she was some invalid or small child who couldn't look after herself. He kept trying to get her to open up, to talk to him as if he was some shrink. All she wanted was to be left alone. She didn't want to talk about her problems. Would that put her face back to the way it was? Would opening up make it so she would be able to film the movie she'd worked so hard to get? Granted, she hadn't been in L.A. for long, but she'd used connections and fought for what she wanted.

Added to that, would talking get her fifty thousand to help support her family?

No. So she wasn't going to waste her time pouring her heart out. Yes, she was bitter, and yes, she was going to lash out at whoever tried to pry inside her heart right now. She just didn't have that chipper energy she was known for. She feared she might never be that happy girl again. Even the spark of attraction they'd had before was out of her reach. And there wasn't a thing she could do about it.

"Have you called your family?" he asked as he maneuvered through the traffic.

"No."

Their phone was probably still shut off, but she would send her brother a text in a few days. Even though he was away at college, he usually went home on weekends if he was able to get off work from his part-time job.

On the other hand, she might not text him at all. Why would she want them to know she'd failed? She'd been so, so close and had lost it all. She refused to text her sister, whom she rarely talked to, anyway. The woman was too busy with her perfect family in Texas to be bothered with helping.

She tried to swipe at the moisture in her eyes, reaching up with her right arm.

"Ouch. God," she groaned.

"Take it easy." Noah reached over and patted her leg. "I know it's habit to use your right arm, but try to hold it still. The more you rest it, the sooner it will heal."

"I don't care about my arm," she told him. "That's the least of my concerns."

He drove for a moment before breaking the silence again. "This will get better, Callie. I know you don't see that proverbial light at the end of the tunnel, but it's there. We need to give this some time."

"We?" she mocked. "I'm positive your career will go on, Noah. You have everything you could ever want."

His hands tightened around the steering wheel. "We all have our own hell, Callie. I've just learned to live with mine."

Callie doubted very much his *hell* was life-changing. He probably had to pay more property taxes or didn't get invited to some of his clients' glamorous parties. No matter what the so-called darkness in his life was, Callie knew it couldn't compare to having her dreams slide through her fingers like sand. She'd held that reality for such a short time and now she would have nothing to show for it.

"I don't mean to argue with you," he told her softly. "I'm here to help you and that's exactly what I'm going to do."

"I still don't think staying with you is the answer," she told him.

"If you have a better suggestion, I'm all ears."

She sighed and ignored the twinge of pain in her shoulder at the deep breath. "I hate being someone's responsibility and an inconvenience."

"Callie, you're neither of those things. If I didn't want to help, I wouldn't have volunteered. Besides, you need assistance and I'm a doctor. You're getting the best free of charge."

She never dreamed if she ever got an invitation to Noah's Beverly Hills home it would be for him to play doctor in the literal sense. There would be no way he'd ever want to date her now. What man would find a woman with a slash down her face attractive? She hadn't even talked to Noah about surgery, but she highly doubted she'd ever look the same again.

She'd worked in his office long enough to know that scars could never be fully removed—minimized, yes, but it would still be there. Even with microdermabrasion or, God forbid, a skin graft, there would still be a slight imperfection on her face. And Noah Foster was used to perfection—that was his job, for crying out loud.

She rested her head against the back of the seat and let the silence of the car surround her. She didn't feel like chitchatting, didn't feel like thinking positively as he'd suggested. Surely she was entitled to a pity party, right? Entitled or not, she was throwing one for herself. Hopefully, when they arrived at his house, he'd leave her alone to wallow in her misery.

A short while later he pulled into a gated drive, rolled down his window and punched in a sequence of numbers until the wrought-iron gate slid to the side, allowing them through. A large, two-story, beige stucco home, with white trim and white columns surrounding the arched entryway, took center stage in the circular drive. Noah hit the garage-door opener and eased the car inside.

"I'll come around and help you out."

Since Callie didn't have the energy or the will to fight, she allowed Noah to escort her into the house. Normally she would've taken the time to marvel at the spacious, pristine kitchen, but she just wanted to go to her room…wherever it was located.

"You'll be upstairs with me." He led the way as he rolled her small suitcase behind him. "I meant, beside me."

Fantastic. Now she was not only in his house out of pity and obligation, she was going to have to sleep with one wall separating them. As if any lingerie would override her mummified state. Sheer material was sexy…sheer gauze, not so much.

"I can show you where your room will be, then you can do what you want." He moved up the wide, curved staircase that circled around a low-hanging chandelier. "I can fix lunch while you unpack, if you'd like."

Once at the top of the steps, she stopped. "Noah," she said, waiting until he turned. "You don't have to do this. Other than changing my bandages and helping me with basics because of my collarbone, pretend I'm not here. You don't have to feed me or entertain me."

He left the suitcase and stepped toward her. Placing his hand on her good shoulder, he looked into her eyes. There was that mesmerizing gaze that had made her toes curl, her belly tingle, so many times. And now was no different. But in so many ways, the important ways, this instance was nothing like the others.

The last time he'd touched her and looked into her eyes. he'd kissed her with so much passion, so much desire....

"Pretending you're not here would be impossible," he told her, holding her gaze. "I know you aren't comfortable, but it's me, Callie. We've worked together long enough, and went quite a big step beyond friendship in my car the other day, that I'd hoped you would be comfortable here. This doesn't have to be difficult. Let me care for you. Please."

She couldn't keep looking at him. She almost felt like a kid, like if she looked away, maybe he couldn't see her. Her eyes darted to the V in the neck of his black T-shirt.

"What are you thinking right now?" he asked.

With her one working shoulder, she shrugged beneath his touch.

He took his free hand and tipped her chin up so she was looking at him once more. "Talk to me, Callie. I won't let you go through this alone, even though you want to."

Blinking back tears, she sighed. "I just don't know how you can look at me like that."

"Like what?"

"Like...like you care for me."

His head tipped to the side as he smiled. "Callie, I do care for you or you wouldn't be here. You're hurt and it's my fault."

Confused, Callie stepped to the side, away from his touch. "What do you mean, your fault?"

"If I hadn't asked you to model, you wouldn't have been on that freeway and you wouldn't have been in the accident."

She hadn't thought it possible to hurt more, but pain sliced through every fiber of her being. His declaration just proved she was at his house, under his care, because he felt pity. And not just pity, but obligation and guilt, and not because they'd begun something in the car the other day.

She closed her eyes, forcing the tears back until she was alone. "Just show me to my room. I'm tired."

He looked as if he wanted to say more, but after hesitating a brief moment, he nodded and moved farther down the wide hallway. Callie prayed her collarbone would recover fast so she could go home.

For so long she'd been such a fighter. But right now, she wasn't so sure she had any fight left in her.

She wanted to have something to push toward, to look forward to after her healing was over. But she knew the odds of living out her dream had more than likely died the second her car slammed into that semi. And Callie would replay that hellacious moment in her head over and over until she died. Of that she was dead sure.

She headed to bed, praying somehow things would look better in the morning.

Five

Noah put the towels away in his master suite and glanced at the small picture of Malinda and him during one of their earlier, carefree times that sat on a shelf beside the window. This was the only picture in the house he hadn't stored in a box on a shelf in the back of his closet. One last reminder of the happiest moments of his life.

He still had a closet full of clothing from Malinda's job as a personal shopper; most of them still had tags. But for some reason he still couldn't let go.

Some reason? No, he knew the reason. How could he let go? If he let go of the past, he'd be finalizing the fact that he had failed the one person he'd loved more than life itself. If he severed all ties with that portion of his life, the finality of the truth would settle in deeper, and quite possibly cripple him.

He just couldn't bear to face the truth. Not only was Malinda gone, he hadn't been able to do anything to stop her swift spiral down to the depths of her drug overdose.

And Callie thought he knew nothing of hell on earth? He lived it every single day. The reminder of the life he thought he'd have with Malinda was always in the forefront of his mind. Between the picture he just couldn't take down and tending to Thelma's needs, the past just wouldn't let him go. He was caught in the vise of this damn nightmare and he had no way of getting out and moving on. And he feared he'd always be on this roller-coaster ride of emotions.

As he moved into his bedroom, he sighed. He was getting frustrated with Callie and he didn't want to go all alpha male on her and take over, but he would if he saw she wasn't taking care of herself. Stubbornness had no place in the healing process.

Since they'd arrived, she hadn't come out of her room. He'd asked her about eating and she'd claimed she wasn't hungry and just wanted to rest. Well, that was nearly five hours ago.

Now it was time for her medicine, so she was going to have to open the door and let him in. She had to eat something because she couldn't take these heavy pain meds on an empty stomach or she'd feel a whole lot worse. He'd also apply more ointment to her face, though that was really just an excuse to get close to her.

Callie's self-esteem and bubbling energy seemed to have been a casualty in the accident, and he intended to make them come back to life. More than likely that would take time, but Noah couldn't watch another woman destroy herself whether it be via drugs or depression.

As a doctor, he'd vowed to protect and heal people. But as a man, he just couldn't sit by and see Callie beat herself up and let her anger and frustrations fester. If she didn't open up, she might end up worse than she was now.

And yeah, the irony of him thinking someone needed to open up was not lost on him. Looked as if the pot and the kettle would be spending a lot of time butting heads over the next few weeks.

Noah kept Callie's medicine in his room so he could have easy access, but also so it wouldn't be with her. The risk of her becoming addicted was too great. He would let her have the prescription painkillers for the next two days, but after that it would be over-the-counter meds. He needed to wean her off the narcotics.

Just the thought of Callie hooked on painkillers sickened him. But the fact they were back in his house only made him have flash upon flash of another woman, another drug.

Of course, before Callie's accident he'd wondered where all her money was going and he'd even considered the possibility of her using, but he wanted to dismiss those tainted thoughts. His past with Malinda just made him skeptical, and where Callie was concerned, he had a gut feeling what he saw was what he got. Perhaps that was why he found her so refreshing. She'd never tried to be fake and she tended to wear her heart on her sleeve.

Grabbing the antibiotic and the mild painkiller from the top of his chest of drawers, he headed next door to her room. There were five spare bedrooms in his house and for some reason he'd chosen to put her right beside him.

There were so many underlying reasons. He'd told her it was because he wanted to be near in case she needed help, but in actuality, he wanted to be close because this was Callie, and he'd envisioned something more intimate between them. He had ever since she'd come to work for him six months ago.

Now, though, his rational mind told him he had to put that desire on a back burner. It wasn't that the accident had diminished his attraction; he simply realized the timing was off. The man in him, however, could hardly ignore the desire he felt for her.

And now that she was under his roof, he could choose to

either be a man and potential lover or be her doctor and caring friend.

His sense of responsibility made that decision for him.

With the bottles in one hand, he tapped on her door with the other.

Callie looked away from her breathtaking view from the window seat toward the door when Noah knocked. He'd been trying to get her to come out, but she just wasn't in the mood. Besides, this bedroom was the size of her apartment and the view of the pool complete with waterfall and hot tub was rather relaxing to stare at.

"I'm fine, Noah," she called without getting up.

"I need to look at your bandage and I have something for your pain."

Of course he would have to come in. She glanced down to her less-than-sexy attire of black yoga capris and a T-shirt, She only had one arm through because she refused to call for Noah to help her dress. At some point, she feared she'd have to suck it up and let him assist her.

She crossed to the door and pulled it open to see Noah leaning against the doorjamb holding a small container with gauze, tape, ointment and pills. His eyes raked over her appearance.

"Why didn't you tell me you needed help dressing?"

She tilted her chin up. "Because I didn't."

"Don't start this arrangement off by being stubborn and ridiculous."

Instead of retorting, because it would just cause an argument, she eyed his inventory.

"I was just dismissed this morning," she told him. "Surely this doesn't need to be looked at already."

"I want to make sure there's enough antibiotic on it. If it gets too dry, the scar can be harder to repair."

Callie rolled her eyes. "You're not actually thinking this is repairable, are you? I know the odds, Noah."

Noah sat his stuff down on the desk a little harder than he should've and Callie jumped.

"Listen to me," he said, taking her by her one good shoulder. "I am going into this with a positive attitude and you need to, as well. Until or unless I see that your scar is indeed irreparable, we will approach this as if everything is going to be fine. Understand?"

Callie refused to allow the warmth of his strong hand to seep in any farther than her T-shirt. She couldn't let that fantasy of the two of them together come into play just because she was staying at his house…especially because she was staying at his house and he was taking care of her.

"If you want to stay optimistic, go ahead." She stepped away and walked over to the window seat she'd just vacated. "I'm going to be a realist here and try to come up with a plan B."

"What do you mean, plan B?" he asked.

Callie leaned her back against the warm glass and pulled her knees up to rest her feet on the cushion. "I can't very well model for you, act or work in an office that promotes beauty and perfection. And going back home to Kansas is even more depressing, so I need to figure out where to go from here."

Noah crossed the room and took a seat beside her. "The modeling and the acting might be out for now, but who said you can't work in my office? I certainly never said, nor did I imply, that you were going to be replaced. God, Callie, did you think because you have an injury that I'd ask you to leave? I'm sure Marie will be more than happy to cover for you until you're ready to come back to work. Besides, with the other office opening there will be plenty of work."

Callie stared back into those dark, sexy eyes. "I wasn't talking about when my arm heals, Noah. Do you really want your clients to see this ugly, marred face as soon as they come in the door?"

Noah slid a stray hair behind her ear and ran a fingertip down her uninjured cheek. "What I want my clients to see is a woman with a bubbly personality who will put them at ease and make them feel welcome. That's why I hired you to begin with."

Callie rolled her eyes. "Don't lie to me."

"I'm not lying, and I'm not going to let you stay in this room until you're healed to your perfect standards."

"That day will never come," she muttered.

Noah came to his feet and took the hand on her good side. "Come with me."

Callie hesitated until she realized Noah was relentless and he wouldn't back down. The sooner she played his little charade, the sooner he'd leave and she could go back to her self-imposed solitary confinement.

He led her to the adjoining bath and stood her in front of the mirror that spread across the entire wall behind the double sinks. Yeah, as if she wanted to be shoved in front of a mirror.

"Noah, I don't think—"

"Look," he demanded. "Turn and look at your uninjured side."

She moved her head so she could see her smooth, perfectly intact face void of any makeup, marks, scars.

"Now turn and look at the other side."

With a sigh, she turned until she saw that hideous bandage that mocked her and the dreams she'd lost.

"Does this exercise have a point?" she asked.

His eyes met hers in the mirror. "You're the same person, Callie, from the left or the right. Whether you have a bandage, a scar or flawless skin. What you have going on here on the outside doesn't make a difference to who you are on the inside."

Callie laughed because the only other option was to puddle to the floor and cry. "Do you hear yourself? You make your living off making people beautiful and perfect and you're lecturing me on what's on the inside?"

He turned her to face him, but he didn't back up. His strong, hard body held hers against the counter of the vanity. How many times had she wished for a moment like this? How many fantasies had she conjured up after that heated kiss in his car? If only she'd acted on that kiss and taken what he'd been obviously willing to give. But now she'd never know. She'd never have that intimacy with Noah because she wasn't the beautiful woman she used to be. Plain and simple.

"I know you, Callie," he said, holding her gaze only inches away. "I know what you have inside. You're capable of so much more than giving up."

"I'm not giving up," she defended. "I'm taking a break. Of all the times I looked ahead to see my dreams and the obstacles that could get in my way, this was never, ever a thought in my mind."

"Okay, so you've been blindsided." He pushed away that annoying strand of hair that kept sliding from behind her ear. "Don't let this define you. Don't let your insecurities take over and alter your direction in life."

That overweight teen from Kansas started to rear her ugly head. And at this point in time, Callie would almost rather turn back into the chubby, insecure girl she once was as opposed to the woman who might never reach the one goal she'd had her whole life all because of one marred cheek.

"You have no idea what insecurities I hold, Noah. The person who worked for you isn't the same person I used to be."

"The person who worked for me is the real you," he told her. "I don't care who you were before or who you think you are now. I can tell you're a fighter, Callie. I wouldn't admire you so much if you weren't."

Callie's breath hitched. Noah's face was so, so close to hers. Two days ago she would've taken this opportunity and kissed him, not caring about the possible rejection because she would've been confident in his participation.

But now she wasn't even going there. Besides the fact that her whole face was still very sore, she didn't think kissing a mummy was on Noah's Bucket List.

"I agree this is a major speed bump on your path to getting what you want," he went on as if he had no clue where her thoughts were going. "But I'm not going anywhere and we'll get through this. When you're ready for surgery, we'll explore our options on how to make this as quick and efficient as possible."

Callie shook her head. "I don't have that kind of money, Noah. Reconstruction is very expensive. I work on the statements, remember?"

"I'm my own boss. Remember?" he asked with a slight grin. "I meant it when I said I'd stand by you, Callie. I will make sure you have the best reconstruction—and that means me. I won't trust another surgeon to your needs."

"Do I have a say in the matter?"

He shrugged. "Did you want another doctor?"

"Of course not, but don't steamroll me." She sighed, looked up into his eyes and continued, "Why are you taking me on as a charity case? I couldn't possibly repay you."

He took her good hand and held it between his two warm ones. "I'm not looking for payment of any kind. I just want to see you happy. I want to see you reach that dream you so deserve, and I want to make sure you know that I'm here for you and that someone cares enough to look after you."

Callie's eyes filled with tears, and she cursed that constant state of vulnerability she'd felt in the past twenty-four hours. Still, no one had ever said such things to her before.

"I don't deserve you as a friend," she whispered. "I'm

going to be a complete jerk during this process. I'm pretty angry and I don't want you to bear the brunt of that anger. I can be my biggest cheerleader, but I can also be my own worst enemy."

"I'm not worried about myself." He placed a kiss on her forehead. "And I'm not worried about you, either, because I'm not going to let you beat yourself up for something that wasn't your fault."

She leaned into his touch, not caring if she appeared defenseless or weak. Right now she was both and there was no point in hiding the fact.

"I just keep replaying the accident in my mind," she admitted as she sniffled against his shirt. "I saw all the brake lights. I started to get over and that semi literally came out of nowhere."

His hand roamed up and down her back, his chin resting on her forehead. "You don't have to relive it now, Callie. You're safe."

Safe? She'd had nightmares last night while she'd been in the hospital; surprisingly her cries hadn't woken Noah up as he'd slept in the chair near her bed. She prayed the dreams wouldn't visit her again tonight.

"It's impossible not to replay it," she told him, lifting her head to look back into his eyes. "My life changed in literally seconds. There were so many cars in the accident. I heard there were no fatalities, but I feel as if a portion of me died."

"You can't mean that." He cupped her jaw and leaned down closer to her face. "Don't even think like that."

His face was a breath away and he was so angry. She'd read somewhere that passion and anger were similar and one could change to the other in the blink of an eye.

But she was a fool for thinking of passion and an even bigger fool for believing Noah would take this moment and turn it into something sexual.

The muscle ticked in his jaw and Callie knew he was angry so she just nodded.

"I'll go get the supplies."

He stalked out and Callie sighed as she sagged back against the counter. This was going to be a long six weeks of recovery.

Six

Callie took a seat on the small stool in front of the vanity. She wanted to get this doctor/patient time over with. Their bonding moment wasn't something she was comfortable with because she certainly didn't want to give him any more ammunition to fuel his pity.

She'd not only been so close to her dream of landing a role, she'd finally gotten Noah Foster to see her as a desirable woman. Now she didn't even want to know what he thought when he looked at her.

"Sorry." Noah came back in with supplies and a shirt. "I ran to my room to grab this for you."

She eyed the shirt and glanced up at him. "A shirt?"

"It's a button-down," he explained. "You can't keep your one arm tucked beneath a T-shirt for six weeks. This way you won't have to lift your arm over your head. You can just slide it through the sleeve."

That would be more convenient, but if she needed to change, then…

"I can help," he offered.

"No." She sat up in her seat, eyes on him. "I can do it."

"You're going to be stubborn, aren't you?" he asked. "I've seen naked women before."

"Not this naked woman."

His eyes roamed over her, then back up. "Do you think the way we were headed a few days ago that I never would've gotten you naked, Callie?"

Chills spread over her; her skin tingled. She knew exactly where they'd been heading.

"Do you think I wanted to just kiss you like that and leave it?" He stepped closer, just enough for her to have to tilt her head up to keep hold of his warm gaze. "I don't choose lovers on a whim."

"Noah…"

He held up a hand, took a step back and shook his head. "Sorry. That was completely out of line. Let's see what your face looks like."

Callie released the pent-up breath she'd been holding.

Going to his knees on the plush carpet, he slowly eased the surgical tape from her face and below her jaw to examine the wound. "Sorry, I know that pulls."

"It's okay."

She closed her eyes, not because of the pain, but because she couldn't bear to see his face when he looked at her injury. She hadn't let him look at her wound in the hospital. She'd been poked enough, and the last person she wanted playing doctor was her very attractive boss.

Biting the inside of her lips, Callie waited in the silence for anything. A hitch in his breath, a mutter of curse words. Anything to indicate his thoughts.

After a moment without the bandage, she finally opened her eyes, but didn't look at him. "Be honest. I can handle it."

"I'll fix this," he replied, his voice thick.

Callie eased around to look him in the eye. "That's not what I asked. How bad is it? If I were your patient, what would you tell me?"

His eyes met hers. "You *are* my patient. This will take some time. I can't tell you for certain because of the swelling, but if the tissues beneath aren't too damaged, then we have good odds of minimal scarring. I will do everything in my power to make that happen."

Callie held his gaze. "You don't have to do this, Noah."

"I don't trust your care to another surgeon."

"I didn't mean the surgery," she corrected. His face was so close to hers now, but if she thought she was hideous before with her bandages, she was certainly grotesque now without. "I mean take care of me. I know I need someone. I just don't want to be a burden for you."

A smile flirted around his kissable lips. "We've been through this. I'm a doctor and I'm your friend. If I didn't want to help, I wouldn't have offered."

"But you offered out of pity," she told him, hating that damn word and all the emotions it stirred within her.

"I offered because I don't want to see you suffer and I want to make sure you get the proper care." He sighed and turned to grab the ointment. "Now, are you going to let me help or are we still going to argue over the living arrangements for the next several weeks?"

Callie tried to grin, but her face was too sore. "I guess you can win this round."

"You should know by now that I win all the rounds," he told her with a full-fledged, double-dimple grin. "As a doctor and a man."

Callie had to look away. She couldn't fall under his spell

even more than she already had. She couldn't keep wishing
for things that could never be because she didn't think she
could handle any more letdowns.

First things first. Her love life would have to be put on
hold…again. She needed to climb back up and see what happened after she recovered and had surgery on her face. Then,
maybe, if all worked out she could circle back around to where
she and Noah had left off making out in his car. That is, if
he hadn't moved on. What were the chances of him staying
single for weeks, months?

In fact, his personal life seemed to be very hush-hush, so it
must be busy. Anytime she had tried to bring it up to Marie,
she'd gotten the message clearly: his love life was off-limits.
But Callie couldn't imagine what a sexy, young plastic surgeon would keep so secretive.

Noah put away all the supplies once he was done changing
Callie's bandage. She'd taken her medicine and had asked for
some privacy. He was all too happy to oblige.

He shouldn't have forced his way into her room to change
that bandage. She would've been fine until tomorrow, but he
just had to see how she was doing. The doctor in him knew
she was fine, but the man in him, the man who was filled with
guilt, had to keep his eye on her to make sure she was okay.

As he started to head back downstairs, he passed by her
room and heard the hiss of water running.

What the hell?

He knocked on her door, but got no response. Surely she
wasn't actually trying to shower or take a bath. Was she?

He tried her knob, and when it turned beneath his hand,
he eased the door open and called her name. "Callie? Everything okay?"

She didn't answer, but the sound of the Jacuzzi tub filling
with water filtered through from the attached bath.

Damn fool woman. How could she do this on her own with that arm in a sling? Not to mention she couldn't get her stitches wet.

He walked to the open bathroom door and sucked in a breath. Callie stood with her back to him wearing only thin satin panties and her T-shirt, which she was trying to wrestle up her body.

When she cried out in pain, he stepped forward. "Callie, stop."

She jerked around, her eyes wide. "What are you doing in here?"

"I heard the water and thought you'd need help." He willed his eyes to stay on her face and not travel down the path of her toned, tanned legs or to the triangle of pink satin between her thighs. "What the hell are you doing trying to have a bath alone?"

"I thought if I soaked for a while it might help the soreness."

He leaned over and turned the faucets off so he didn't have to keep talking over the water. "It will, but you can't do this on your own, remember? That was the whole reason for having someone care for you."

She eyed the tub, then him. "There's no way you're going to help me take a bath."

The image nearly killed him.

"I need to at least help you out of that shirt and underwear."

He resisted the urge to swipe his damp hands down his jeans. He was a doctor, for crying out loud. He'd seen more naked women than Hugh Hefner, and here he was in his guest suite afraid to see Callie in nothing but a tan. But no matter the near-naked women he'd seen in his office, none of them had been Callie. None of them conjured up emotions, feelings…hormones…the way Callie did.

"Don't make this uncomfortable, Noah." She tried to pull

the hem down lower, hiding her flat stomach and the flash of a jewel in her belly button. "I can take a bath. It may be hard, but I won't overdo it."

"Nothing has to be hard. That's the whole reason you're here."

God, this was infuriating. He stepped forward and reached for the hem of the shirt, but Callie stepped back.

"Noah, I can't do this." Her bottom lip trembled and her eyes filled with tears that nearly dropped him to his knees because he couldn't handle seeing her so hurt. "I'm a horrifying sight, I have bruises all over me and I'm stuck here until I can be alone. Added to that, I can't let go of the memory of us kissing and it's really making staying here, being so close to you, difficult. Please, I'm begging you, let me have what little pride I have left."

Shocked at her declaration, he remained silent. The woman was blunt, truthful, and he admired the hell out of her.

"You can stay in the bedroom. I'll close this door and if I need something I promise to yell." Her chin tilted up as she blinked away the tears. "Can we agree to that?"

Damn, he admired her stubbornness. He had to admit that if the tables were reversed, he'd be pissed to have his independence taken away.

Noah nodded. "I'll be right outside that door, Callie. Be careful not to get the bandage on your face wet or move your arm too much. You can bend at the elbow, but don't lift the entire arm up."

Callie smiled through her watery eyes. "I'll be careful."

Hesitating only a moment, Noah reluctantly left the room and shut the door. With just that piece of wood between them, he leaned against it and closed his eyes.

Callie was so much like Malinda. So strong-willed, so independent and stubborn. Why was he attracted to that type?

And that was just their personality. He didn't even want to

think how their physical attributes were similar. Same long, dark red hair, same milky skin tone.

He could admit to himself that when he'd hired Callie, her looks were just another reason. After all, Malinda had only been gone six months and this was just one more way he could hold on to her.

But the longer Callie worked for him, the more he could see the differences between the two women. Callie laughed more, smiled when she spoke and truly had a gift for making a room brighter simply by walking into it.

Noah listened, waiting for her to call for him, praying she did all the while praying she didn't. He'd go in there in a second if she needed him, but first he'd have to turn on doctor mode. If he went in there as a man—a man attracted to a woman—he'd be a complete jerk and forget about her injured body and take his fill of looking at her, touching her and quite possibly kissing her breathless as he had the other day. God, he wanted his mouth on her again.

And didn't that make him all kinds of a fool for having these thoughts about an injured, vulnerable woman?

He heard the water slosh and his mind filled with the erotic image of her settling into the oversize garden tub.

"Turn the jets on," he yelled through the door. "That will help ease the soreness."

As if he needed another image of her relaxing, now he pictured her with her hair spilling down around her, her head tipped back against the porcelain as the jets brought thousands of bubbles up to the surface.

His phone vibrated in his pocket, but when he checked the caller ID and saw it was his Realtor, he shoved the cell back in. He wasn't in the mood to hear another piddly offer on the house they were trying to sell. The other two offers were laughable; he wasn't selling this home just to get rid of it and he sure as hell wasn't selling it at a loss.

Malinda had chosen this Beverly Hills mansion when they'd decided to move in together. Noah had a home on the other side of town, but this was closer to where she was working as a personal shopper until she caught her "big break." In love and naive, Noah agreed to move, but he loved his other house so much, he held on to it and rented it out.

He still had that home he could go to, but he just couldn't say goodbye to the memories he and Malinda had made here…the happy ones.

Noah swallowed the lump of guilt that always settled in his throat when he thought of how he should've seen the signs of her abuse earlier. How he should've done something…anything. He was a doctor, for pity's sake. His job was to fix people, but the one person he'd loved and had planned to spend his life with he had failed and she had paid the ultimate price.

"Noah?"

He jerked against the door and opened his eyes. "Yes?" he called back.

"Um, it's hard to wash my hair with one hand."

Oh, Lord. He was going to have to go back in there—where she was naked, wet and needy. Noah took a deep breath and shoved aside the man who had wanted Callie's sexy body for months now and he slid his doctor persona into place.

You're a professional, damn it. Act like one.

"Need help?" he asked, gritting his teeth.

"Please."

One simple word. It meant so much and he knew she'd put her pride and dignity aside.

He eased the pocket door open and entered the steamy room.

"I'll need another towel," she explained. "I wanted to cover up so this wouldn't be any weirder."

He glanced her way and sure enough she had draped the

large white bath towel across her. It was tucked beneath her armpits and floated down across her tanned thighs.

He knelt down beside the tub. "Just sit up a tad."

Taking the shampoo bottle, he squeezed a generous amount into his palm and lathered his hands together. When he finally started rubbing his fingers through her long, silky strands, she moaned.

"God, it always feels so good when someone else washes your hair," she said. "I can scrub and massage all day, but it's just not the same at all."

So had her previous boyfriends done this for her? If she was his, and this was the type of thankful reaction she gave, he'd sure as hell wash her hair every damn night.

"I actually tipped the shampoo guy at the salon two weeks ago even more than usual because he massaged my scalp longer."

Noah felt like an idiot. Maybe she wasn't talking about past boyfriends at all. Noah would pretend she was just discussing the salon and not potential foreplay with other men.

"Hang on, I'll grab something to rinse it with."

He came to his feet and shook off the suds into the tub. Beneath the vanity he found a small, plastic pitcher his cleaning lady always used to rinse the shower and tub when she cleaned. He squatted back down and dipped it into the water and began rinsing her hair. Time and time again he dipped and poured. He'd run his hand through her hair to see if he still saw suds, but even when they were long gone, he kept rinsing and running his hand through her long, crimson strands.

The way they splayed across her damp, bare back was sexy. The way she moaned the entire freaking time he washed her hair was sexy. And the fact she sat inches away from him totally naked was beyond sexy. *Torturous* was more the word. He'd never imagined if he ever got the chance to see Callie naked she'd be broken and battered and vulnerable. And in this tub alone.

"Um, Noah?" she peered over her shoulder at him. Water droplets clung to the edge of her thick, dark lashes. "It's rinsed by now, isn't it?"

He squeezed the pitcher in his hand, surprised it didn't pop out and shoot across the room.

"Yeah," he replied, his voice huskier than he would've liked. "It's clean."

Her eyes darted to his mouth, and she might as well have touched him below the belt with her bare hand because the effect was the same. He was hard in a second.

"Thanks," she told him, her eyes locked onto his. "I can take it from here. But if you could get me a dry towel…"

A droplet of water slid down her forehead and Noah reached out and thumbed it away. But he didn't remove his hand. He cupped her cheek and stroked her soft, dewy skin.

"It's not often someone takes my breath away," he whispered. "Hardly ever, actually."

"Noah—"

He eased forward slowly, giving her ample time to stop him. "I can't ignore this," he told her. "I can't pretend you don't stir something in me, Callie. And I sure as hell can't pass this opportunity up."

Her mouth opened beneath his as he caressed her uninjured cheek. Keeping his touch light, he coaxed her mouth open and slid his tongue in to meet hers.

Another of those soft moans escaped her and Noah found it damn hard to resist the urge to haul her out of that tub and find the nearest flat surface.

Callie pulled back and brought her hand to her lips. "Noah, we can't do that."

"Pretty sure we can and did."

"No, I mean, we can't do this." She waved her good hand

between them. "You don't need this complication on top of caring for me, and I can't afford to be sidetracked by you and your charms and those kisses. You make me all muddled and I can't think when you touch me."

He couldn't help but grin. At least she wasn't crying or angry over the accident. Apparently he'd found just the thing to distract her. But at what price? Now he was more tortured than ever. But sacrificing himself for her was a no-brainer. He'd do anything to make her smile again, make her whole again.

"Glad I could take your mind off your problems for a moment," he told her.

Callie eased back into the tub. "Did you kiss me because—"

"No." He held up a hand. "Kissing you had nothing to do with this accident. I kissed you before and I plan on kissing you again. One has nothing to do with the other. I like kissing you, Callie. And if it helps, I can barely think when your mouth is on mine, so this sexual attraction goes both ways."

She closed her eyes. "But I just don't think this is right, Noah. I don't want you to feel because we're thrown together like this it means that we should be intimate."

Noah came to his feet, pointing down to his bulging zipper. "You think this didn't happen before you came here? I assure you, many times at work I'd have to go to the restroom or my office and close the door and recite the Gettysburg Address to get my mind off you."

Callie raised her brows as her gaze darted from his erection to his face. "You did not recite the Gettysburg Address— Are you admitting that you've wanted me for a while?"

"Yes, I did and yes, I am."

Callie adjusted her wet towel. "Well, um, that's… I can't think right now, Noah. You caught me at a weak moment and

I'm on drugs. Is this how you get women into your bed?" she joked.

The band of guilt around Noah's chest tightened. He turned toward the linen closet and grabbed another towel and sat it on the edge of the garden tub.

"Get dressed and we'll see about dinner."

And before he could get too wrapped up in his past or his present, Noah fled the room like a child who was scared of the boogeyman. Because, let's face it, that boogeyman that kept chasing him was himself. No one else was to blame for the death of Malinda.

Seven

Callie tried, she really did try to put on a bra, but it just wasn't going to happen. It wasn't as if her B-cup breasts needed restraints, anyway. She certainly wasn't some busty Playboy type and she wasn't saggy, thank God, so fighting with a bra was not only painful, it was also insane.

Okay, so that was the only perk—bad pun intended—of being injured.

Well, unless she counted the bath she'd just somewhat shared with Noah. The bath *and* the kiss. Mercy, her entire body had heated.

But what on earth had happened afterward? He'd gone pale before he'd grabbed her towel and demanded she dress. She knew he hadn't gone far, in case she needed him, because she could hear him out in the bedroom talking on the phone. She actually had heard him shout to someone about the price being set to sell and he wasn't "giving the damn thing away." Apparently, he was trying to sell his home and not having much luck.

God, what she wouldn't give for a home like this. Her entire threadbare apartment could fit in the guest suite.

After she carefully got into the button-down shirt Noah had loaned her, she used her good hand to pull on a pair of cotton shorts.

She glanced into the mirror. Her hair hung in long, crimson-colored wet ropes, her face was pale, patched and swollen, she wore a blue dress shirt that was so large the shoulder seams nearly hung to her elbows, and she had on hot-pink shorts. Yeah, she wasn't going to be winning any fashion awards with this hot mess.

Realizing she was fighting the proverbial losing battle, Callie grabbed her sling and went into her temporary bedroom. Noah was standing by the window looking out into the yard, his hands fisted at his sides.

"Everything okay?" she asked.

He turned and for a brief second she saw pain lurking behind those stunning gray eyes. He quickly covered the emotions with a smile. "Great. Need help with that?" he asked, nodding to her sling.

"Yeah, I didn't think I could reach and fasten it."

He closed the gap between them and moved her hair out of the way to slide the strap around her neck.

"Sorry," she told him, tilting her head to get her hair out of the way. "I couldn't pull it up or comb it. I'm afraid it's going to be quite a mess until I can use my arm again."

Noah stepped back. "I can comb your hair, Callie. I could probably pull it up, too, but I can't guarantee how good it would look."

Callie stared up at him. For some reason the image of a man combing a woman's hair had always seemed sexy to her. She and Noah had shared an intense moment in the bathroom, so adding hair into the mix wasn't going to do any more damage to her hormones. She didn't think she could want this man any more than she already did.

"If you don't mind." She went to her bag and pulled out a wide-toothed comb. "Use this. My hair is pretty tangly."

He motioned for her to sit on the bed, and once she was settled, he took a seat behind her. His knees rested on either side of her hips and she tried to block out the fact they were both on the bed, she wasn't wearing a bra and they'd just had a major intimate moment in the bathroom.

"It helps if you go in sections," she told him, trying to reach back and part her hair with her left hand. "Otherwise it's more of a mess."

"I think I can figure this out," he told her. "Just tell me if I hurt you."

Yeah, as if she'd tell him that. She didn't want to give him a reason to stop or move away. He combed with ease, taking small sections at a time. Normally when Callie combed her hair she gave it several yanks and if the tangle didn't come free, then the entire knot of hair broke off, but she was surprised and turned on even more at the care Noah was using.

His body seemed to be all around her. Those strong thighs rubbed against her sides as his knees eased forward, his hands in her hair, occasionally brushing against her neck and her cheek as he combed out the tangles.

"I heard you on the phone," she said, trying to ease the sexual tension. "I didn't mean to eavesdrop, but you seemed upset. Anything you want to talk about?"

His hands stilled in her hair a second before he spoke. "Just something I need to deal with that I'm not sure I'm ready for."

"Are you selling your house?" she asked, tracing her fingertip along the damask pattern of the silk comforter.

"Trying to."

"You have somewhere else you'd like to live?"

"I have another house on the other side of town." He shifted his weight on the bed and moved to work on the other side of her hair. "I had been renting it out, but I'm thinking of moving back in there. It's sat empty for a few months."

"Why not sell that one and stay here since all of your stuff is here?"

Noah cleared his throat. "Are you feeling better since your bath?"

O-kay. Apparently, that was a touchy subject.

"That wasn't subtle." She didn't mind stepping into his personal space. After what they'd shared during her bath, personal space seemed to have gone by the wayside. "You seem upset and I'd like to help."

"I know. There are just some things I'm not comfortable discussing with anyone."

There was a story there, but in all honesty, it wasn't her place to pry.

"So are you feeling less sore?" he asked again.

"I'm still sore, but I feel much more relaxed."

"That's good." He eased off the bed and came to his feet. "Where's a rubber band?"

She pointed to her overnight bag. "In there. I have a small travel bag sitting on top. Rubber bands are in that."

He unzipped her bag and grinned. "You're a reader?"

She glanced over to see him holding a mystery. "I love it," she told him. "Nothing like escaping your problems and reading about someone else's."

Noah laughed. "Too bad that's not possible in real life."

She wanted to question him but realized that was prying again, so she remained silent and waited for him to come back with a band.

"How do you want it?" he asked.

Glancing over her shoulder, she laughed. "Seriously? You tell me it won't look good and you think I'll give you specifications? I'm just happy you combed it and it won't look like a nest."

He gathered the sides back and pulled her hair together in the middle at the nape of her neck and wrapped the band around her hair. "I think we'll do the most basic. By the time these weeks are over I may have you wearing a French twist."

"You know what a French twist is?" she asked, surprised.

"I'm not a moron," he joked. "Just because I know the term doesn't mean I know how to do one. But maybe I'll look up hairstyles since I'll not only be your doctor, I'll be your beautician, as well."

Callie laughed, came to her feet and stared down at him. "Yeah, if this plastic-surgeon gig doesn't work out, you can add stylist to your resume. I'll be a reference for you."

He grinned up at her and her heart flipped. She didn't want to enjoy being here this much, because this was temporary. Not only that, if she liked it, she'd have to think of the reason she was actually staying here, and it wasn't pleasant.

"Are you hungry?" he asked as his eyes floated down from her face, landed on her perky nipples and back up.

Oh, she was hungry, and she had a feeling he wasn't just referring to food, either.

She cleared her throat. "I could eat."

"Let's head down to the kitchen and see what we can find."

Yeah, getting out of this bedroom was an excellent idea. Her hormones had obviously not taken a hit in the accident, because they were working just fine.

Noah pounded his heavy bag and tried to block out the image of last night when Callie came from the bathroom, skin still dewy, wet hair clinging to her—no, his—shirt, making the material thinner, making those unconfined breasts all the more enticing...

These next few weeks were going to kill him. Literally flat-out kill him.

As if his sexual pull for her hadn't been strong before, now being under the same roof with her was really testing his willpower.

She'd been here such a short time and already she'd left her mark. Her floral scent filled every room, making him realize having a female in his home was a major milestone.

Callie was the first woman Noah had brought home since the death of Malinda. He'd been on a few dates, but he'd never brought another woman here. This was the home he'd planned to share with his wife, and bringing other women here just didn't seem like the right thing to do.

But Callie's situation was different and he refused to feel guilty for helping a friend…even if she was a friend he was fighting an attraction to. Fighting and failing.

The burn in his knuckles with each punch only helped slightly to keep his mind off the fact his house wasn't selling, the fact that Thelma might or might not be getting the proper meds, and the fact that his new housemate was sexy as hell and walking around wearing his shirt, no bra and shorts that showcased her tanned, toned legs and dainty feet with pink, polished toes. Even the bandage, sling and spattering of purple bruises didn't diminish her beauty. Oh, all of that dulled the light in her eyes, but he'd find a way to put it back.

His cell rang, cutting off the image of Callie parading barefoot through his home as if she belonged. Yanking off his boxing gloves, he moved to the weight bench and grabbed his phone.

"Hello."

"Hey, you busy? You sound winded."

Noah took a seat on the bench and rested his elbows on his knees. "Beating the heavy bag. What's up, Max?"

"Calling to check on Callie. How's she doing?"

Noah sighed. "She's only been here a day. Her injuries were making her sore yesterday, and this morning when she woke she was pretty stiff."

"And you stayed home to play doctor?" Max joked. "Sorry, bad pun. Seriously, dude, are you staying with her today?"

Noah nodded as if his friend could see. "I actually rescheduled all of this week's appointments. I wanted to be able to stay with her for a while until I could see how she was getting along."

"You can't keep your eye on her all the time, Noah." Max hesitated before going on. "You also can't blame yourself for her condition."

"I can do whatever the hell I want," Noah countered, ready to defend his actions. "I won't have another woman suffer when I can prevent it."

Max sighed. "I won't argue with you about this again. I just called to see if you'd like to get together for a cookout or something. I want you to meet Abby."

"Abby?" Noah laughed. "Weren't you just dating someone else?"

"Not dating…"

"Forget it," Noah said. "Bring whomever you want, but let me get back to you as to when. I don't want to make Callie uncomfortable."

He had a feeling the last thing she'd want was visitors, especially a woman of Max's choosing, because if Max was "dating" someone, she more than likely would show up with three things: silicone, implants and a spray tan.

"You know, why don't you just come over?" Noah asked. "I'd love to meet your new friend, but maybe not with Callie around. She's pretty vulnerable right now."

"Sure. I understand. Why don't I come over tomorrow night with some steaks and we can just grill out?"

"I'll run it by Callie, but I'm sure it'll be fine."

"Just text me and let me know what's going on."

"Will do."

Noah hung up and grabbed a towel off the bar to wipe his head and chest. He'd pounded the bag for nearly thirty minutes and before that he'd run five miles on his treadmill. Normally he'd run outside, but he didn't want to leave Callie in case she needed something.

No matter what Max said, Noah knew Callie was his responsibility. She'd been in that accident because of him and she was going to get the proper care because of him, too. It was the least he could do.

Fantasizing about her, thinking about her in a sexual way was not going to help matters. He needed to keep in mind what happened last time he lost himself to a woman who had stars in her eyes.

No, this time he would remain professional. He was one of the best plastic surgeons in L.A., damn it, and he needed to remember that and keep his hormones in check.

He'd just come to his feet when he felt Callie step into the room. He couldn't explain it, but suddenly there was this… presence that had him turning.

She stood leaning against the doorjamb with her good shoulder. "I was wondering if I could use your computer. I forgot to bring my laptop."

He took in the sight of her still sporting his shirt, the one she'd slept in, and those damn sexy legs peeking out beneath little shorts, and like a hormonal, stuttering teenager, he merely nodded.

"Is something wrong?" she asked.

Yeah, something was wrong. He was getting confused between being a man and being a doctor, not to mention the fact he was torn between being dutiful and giving in to his most basic of desires.

"Just trying to finish my workout," he told her, coming

off a little more agitated than he meant to. "I'll be done in a minute."

She straightened. "I won't bother you again."

Turning, she eased back down the hall and disappeared around the corner. Great, now he'd upset her and made her feel worse. As if she needed to feel worse. The woman had lost her dream job, her independence and the simple life she was used to, and he'd growled at her simply because he had a hard-on that he couldn't keep under control.

Well, whose fault was that?

Noah shoved his hands back into his boxing gloves. He wasn't done with that heavy bag. As long as his past demons were chasing him and his present situation was joining in, he needed to punch out some of his anger and frustrations.

Eight

Callie booted up the computer that sat in a small nook off the kitchen. She'd just wanted to look for some online work she could do until she felt comfortable facing the world again. There was no way she could go back to the office looking like a constant work in progress, and there was certainly no way she could go to a casting call, unless they were doing a horror film.

But she wasn't going to focus on what she couldn't do. In order to get back on her feet, she needed to focus on what she could do. Noah wanted to see that old Callie back, so she was going to try.

There were no guarantees, but she had to do something positive. That was the only way she could get out of this house. So far she'd been here for nearly twenty-four hours and she'd had enough of the roller coaster of humiliation and desire to last her a lifetime. Between the bath, the hair and just now seeing him in all his shirtless, sweaty glory, she knew she needed to get some distance.

No, it wasn't smart to try to leave, but if she could find something to do from home using a computer, surely she could stay by herself. She wasn't an invalid; she just had problems getting dressed and bathing. If she worked from home, she wouldn't have to worry about all that.

But even if Noah insisted she stay, she still felt she needed to pay her way somehow. Not to mention the fact she couldn't just take a break from her income. Not only did she have bills to pay for herself, she needed to send some money back home so her parents' phone could be turned back on.

She did have a tiny bit left in savings and she probably should keep it since her future was so unclear, but she couldn't stand the thought of being out of touch.

After a few clicks, she'd taken money from her account and put it into her parents', which she had access to. Then she sent an awkward, left-handed text to her brother so he could get the message to their mom and dad.

Callie did several searches, hoping with her teaching degree she could find something. Maybe online tutoring. That would be ideal.

She'd come to L.A. in the hopes of not using her teaching degree because she'd been so afraid she'd get stuck in a rut. At least as a receptionist, she'd known she wouldn't feel guilty leaving that job when she caught her big break. Working with kids, she would've gotten attached and been worried about leaving midyear.

Thankfully, she'd worked part-time in a dentist's office back home, so she'd had a little experience to get her this job with Noah.

"What are you doing?"

Callie jumped and turned in her chair. Now Mr. Sweaty Rippling Muscles stood just behind her and she hadn't heard him come in. Lord, it was hard to focus when that chiseled, delectable body was staring back at her.

"Looking for an online job," she told him, forcing her eyes to stay locked onto his.

"What the hell for?" he asked, taking his small white hand towel and mopping his forehead. "Is this your way of turning in your resignation?"

Callie came to her feet and winced. The soreness was so much worse today. But she didn't think another intimate bath encounter was such a good idea.

"I didn't figure you'd want a mummy for your reception-ist," she told him, easing back down onto the chair because it was much more comfortable than standing in pain. "Besides, I'm not sure I'll be comfortable around too many people once this bandage comes off."

"How much pain medication have you had?" he asked.

"Enough that I shouldn't feel like this," she told him. "But I guess it would be worse if I hadn't taken those two pills."

"Two?"

"One wasn't cutting it and I just took another before I came to find you. It should kick in soon, I hope."

"I had them in my bedroom."

"I know. They were sitting on your dresser so I grabbed one."

And forced herself not to stare at his bed and wonder...

Okay, so she'd stared and fantasized, but only for a few minutes.

The muscle in Noah's jaw ticked. "You can't take any more medication without asking me first. You only needed one."

"You're not the one in pain," she retorted. "I am and I needed another. You're not my mother."

"No, I'm your doctor and I will flush those pills next time you pull a stunt like that."

Callie had never seen him angry. Frustrated, agitated and

annoyed, yes, but never this angry and never directed toward her. He was practically shaking with waves of fury.

"Okay, okay. Calm down," she told him, holding her hand up. "I'm hoping when it kicks in I'll feel like resting. I didn't sleep too well last night."

"Why didn't you come get me?"

Callie laughed and leaned back against the seat. "What for? Just because I was up didn't mean you had to be. Nothing you could've done."

"You wouldn't have been lonely."

Yeah, she would've. Because no matter what he would've done or said, she would've known he was only sitting with her out of guilt and pity. She'd take loneliness any day over that.

"I was fine. Tired, but fine."

He stared at her for several long moments before he glanced beyond her to the screen. "You're not seriously going to leave the office, are you?"

Callie nodded. "I think I should. It's not fair to you for me to take time off until I heal, and I can't afford the break in income."

"I can help you financially until you're back to work, Callie. I don't want to lose you."

He didn't want to lose her. That warmed her in so many ways, but he wasn't talking on a personal level. More than likely he didn't want to train anyone to fill her shoes and Marie couldn't do both offices.

"Marie, I'm sure, would fill in until you found someone," she told him, only to be rewarded with a scowl.

"I need to call her anyway to let her know how you're feeling because she left me a voice mail."

Callie shook her head. "Talk to her all you want, but I won't be coming back, Noah."

"I need you, Callie."

She jerked up out of her seat, standing literally toe-to-toe with him. The elbow of her arm in the sling bumped against his hard abs.

"You need?" she mocked. "Let me tell you what I need. I need to go back in time, I need to not have this new life I'm adjusting to and I need to get my independence back. Your needs are irrelevant at the moment."

Noah stared at her, his eyes holding on to hers, and Callie wondered if she'd totally overstepped her bounds shouting at not only her boss that way, but also the man who was putting aside his life to help her recover.

She closed her eyes and sighed. "God, I'm sorry. That was really cruel of me to say and very selfish."

Noah's strong hand cupped her cheek. "It's okay. You're entitled to be upset, to hate me, this situation, your life. I'm tough, Callie. I can take it."

She lifted her lids, though her eyes burned with unshed tears. "But you shouldn't have to take it. I just get so frustrated when I look at long-term goals because I can't even put my own clothes on, for pity's sake."

His thumb stroked across her cheek as he glanced down to her lips and back up to her eyes. "I don't mind, Callie. I know it's upsetting to lose your independence, but there's nothing about helping you that bothers me. What does bother me is how hard you are on yourself."

"I just want to be whole again," she told him. "But that may never be."

He wrapped an arm around her waist, tugging her in closer. "It will be if I have anything to say about it."

His lips came down on hers in a powerful yet tender way. Callie froze for a second, but then slid her hand up his bare, sweaty arms. That hard body pressed against hers, combined with his musky scent from his workout, made her moan as his lips continued to claim hers.

She squeezed his thick biceps, making sure to keep her

body angled so she could still get the maximum benefit of rubbing against his even while protecting her arm.

His lips were just as gentle yet demanding as the other night. He nipped at her and pulled her bottom lip between his before he eased back.

Noah rested his forehead to hers and sighed. "I won't apologize for that, Callie. I just can't control myself sometimes around you. I know you're here to heal, not to get mauled, but you do something to me."

"Yeah, you do something to me, too," she admitted.

That something was tying her up in knots and leaving her confused. This man could have nearly any woman he wanted and he was standing in his kitchen—wearing only gym shoes and running shorts with those glorious sweaty pecs on display—and he was kissing a broken woman. That made no sense.

"I can't help but feel you're recovering from something, too." She searched his face. "I may be far off the mark, but sometimes you get this look in your eyes like you're hurt. I've seen it when we discussed the house and when you think I'm not looking."

His eyes closed for the briefest of moments before he opened them and sighed. "I'm going to hop in the shower. Think about what I said and don't start looking for another job just yet."

Callie nodded, unable to form a coherent thought after that kiss and his intense stare as he totally dodged her analysis. Which just proved she was more than likely accurate in her assessment.

Someone or something had a hold on him. He had a past that haunted him and she had a sinking feeling in her stomach that he was waging an inner war with himself. One second he was kissing her like he needed her air in his lungs and the next second his eyes held pain and doubt.

This was so much more than casual. Casual was what had almost transpired before the accident. What was happening now was something even he couldn't explain. Were these higher levels of emotion stemming from their living arrangements? Were they growing closer without even trying, simply because of the accident?

"Oh, I almost forgot. Max called and wanted to know about coming over tomorrow and grilling out. I told him I'd run it by you."

Callie tilted her head. "You don't have to run anything by me, Noah. This is your house."

"I didn't want you to feel uncomfortable."

Nearly every conversation with this man left her heart melting more and more. The way he'd put every single one of her needs first made her wonder what it would be like if he cared for her beyond friendship, beyond the path that was leading them to intimacy.

"I'll be fine," she assured him. "It'll be nice to have something to look forward to."

"I'll let him know." He kissed her forehead. "Now I'm going to take that shower."

After Noah walked away, she sank back into the chair and replayed his previous words. More than once he'd admitted that she affected him. More than once they'd shared heated stares and all-too-brief kisses. But what did all of that mean? Where did he want to go from here?

Callie didn't know, but she did know that she needed to be on her guard where her heart was concerned. She couldn't focus on healing if she was worried about what those kisses meant and what his true feelings were.

She wanted so badly for him to open up and let her in even though his past wasn't her business. And he probably wasn't opening up about this past because they both knew she wasn't going to be part of his future.

* * *

Noah hung up the phone and slid his cell back into his pocket. This evening was going rather smoothly. He and Callie had shared a nice meal on the patio and they'd chatted about mundane things, and he was sure to steer the topic far away from anything sexual because it was all he could do to sit there and watch her as a doctor should watch a patient.

But that kiss in the kitchen earlier had been anything but professional. For the life of him, though, he hadn't been able to stop and he didn't care about the consequences. With her parading around in his oversize shirts… His gut clenched just thinking of it. Now when he went to wash them, they would have Callie's scent all through them.

His emotions were a jumbled, chaotic mess. He'd told himself in the beginning to just be a friend or a doctor, to distance himself from her emotionally. But the more Callie was around him, the more he found he wanted to be around her. So, okay. Sexual chemistry was definitely one thing he could handle. But they hadn't had sex.

Where the hell did that leave his emotional state? Because right now he truly had no clue how to feel or act with her.

He'd been taken so off guard when Callie had mentioned something hurting him, something that still had a hold on him. She'd been spot-on and that fact made him very uncomfortable. Was he that transparent? After a year of living without Malinda he'd thought he'd taken control of his emotions.

Yes, Callie had initially reminded him of Malinda, and even so, he'd believed they could have a short, no-strings affair. But he knew better now. He didn't want his past and present to collide. He was doing all he could to keep from claiming Callie in his bed. Getting wrapped up in another vulnerable woman was not a good idea, especially when that woman could get under his skin as Callie seemed able to do, but his hormones weren't getting that message. He could handle sex, if that was all there was to this relationship, but he had a feeling Callie was thinking of much more…especially now that they'd played house for a few days.

He rubbed the back of his neck and headed back inside. Callie had already gone in, but when his real-estate agent had called, he'd stepped out onto the shaded patio. There was a buyer interested in looking at the house tomorrow afternoon and Noah had agreed to a time. Now he had to get Callie out of the house and maybe persuade her to have a picnic or something in the park. She wouldn't be a fan of going out in public so soon, but there was no other choice.

Noah found her sitting in the living room fumbling left-handed with the remote.

"Let me get that," he told her as he stepped down into the sunken living area. "What do you want to watch?"

She shrugged. "Doesn't matter. I was looking for a good movie, but you have like two thousand channels and I wasn't even sure where to look."

Noah laughed and flopped down beside her. "Name a movie you'd like to see and I'll put it on for you."

She pursed her lips and wrinkled her nose as if in thought. "Hmm…how about *Blackhawk Down?*"

Surprised, Noah grinned. "Really? Why that one? I would've pegged you for a romantic-comedy type."

She shook her head. "Growing up I was a daddy's girl and whatever he watched, I watched. He was a war-movie or Western guy, so that's my thing. Besides, after really researching films and sinking my teeth into the fact that's what I wanted to do, I appreciate all the special effects more."

He placed his hand on her leg. "I'm sorry, Callie."

"It's okay," she told him, her eyes on his hand on her bare thigh. "We're moving forward. Let's just concentrate on right now. Okay?"

He squeezed her leg and went to search for the movie before his hand got a mind of its own and started wandering.

"Sure, come in and hit three buttons and make it look simple," she joked once the movie appeared on the screen. "I was in here for fifteen minutes and got nowhere."

"It's my TV." He grinned and caught the wide smile on her delicate face. "I pretty much know how to work it."

As the movie's opening music started, he propped his feet up onto the squat table in front of him. "So, you liked Westerns and war movies as a kid. Tell me what else you liked."

Callie eased back against the arm of the sofa, sitting somewhat sideways. Noah reached over and slid a hand beneath her thighs to bring her legs up and over his lap. He didn't know why he did that, but he wanted that additional innocent contact with her. Granted, this wasn't so innocent considering where his thoughts were heading.

"Well, I wasn't really popular in school so I was more of a homebody."

Noah jerked back. "Not popular? How is that possible? You're outgoing, not to mention stunning."

He cringed at the same time she did and he knew he'd chosen the wrong words.

"Damn, Callie. I just keep digging that hole deeper." He shook his head and met her gaze. "Even though you've had this setback, you're still beautiful to me."

She smiled and rested her head on the back cushion. "That's okay. It's not your fault. It is what it is."

"I plan on taking you to the office next week if you don't mind."

Her eyes widened. "What for?"

"A minor microdermabrasion. Your stitches will come out and I'd like to start removing some of the dead skin a little at a time and take this process slowly so we can insure the best results."

Callie smiled. "That would be great, Noah. The sooner I can see what I'm dealing with, the better."

Pleased with her eagerness, he settled deeper into the cushions and rested his arms on her legs. "So, what did you do at home since you didn't participate in school activities?"

"My dad found this old pool table at a yard sale and worked to clean it up. We loved that thing. Every night my brother and I would bet who would win. I beat him nearly every time."

Noah laughed. "I can see that. You're a fighter."

Her eyes held his. "You're right. Sometimes I forget that." She offered a smile.

"You're entitled to, but just make sure you don't lose it."

"I won't."

Her eyes darted to the big screen as the movie began. He watched her for a moment before he, too, rested his head against the back of the couch and slid his hand down to one of her dainty feet. He began massaging one foot, working her arch, her heel, each of her tiny toes.

She let out a slight moan and he smiled as he picked up the other foot. As she watched her movie, her body relaxed and Noah kept right on massaging her. He wanted her to stay relaxed, wanted her to stay comfortable.

By the time the movie was about halfway through, Noah glanced over and found her asleep. He'd stopped massaging her a while ago, but apparently she'd settled into this state of comfort and let her guard down.

With her slinged arm resting on her stomach and her other arm behind her as a pillow, she looked so innocent, so young. She had bluish circles beneath her eyes and he knew she hadn't been sleeping well. She was worried about her prospective career and he'd be lying if he didn't agree that her future in the movie industry was unstable.

But he also hadn't been lying when he said he'd do everything in his power to make her whole again. He'd make damn sure she had the best treatment and care she needed, and he'd be with her every step of the way.

He slid a hand over her foot, over her ankle and along her shin. She was so soft, so smooth. His hand glided back down as his groin tightened.

God, what a jerk he was sitting here getting hard and stroking a sleeping woman. Seriously? Had it come to that because he couldn't just admit how much he wanted her and instead let fear prevent him from acting on his emotions? Had he turned into a voyeur?

Her lids fluttered and Noah watched as she awoke and her gaze met his. Slowly she pulled her arm from behind her head and extended it before laying it across her stomach.

Darkness had long since settled, and the only light came from the big flat screen hanging on the wall across the room. Her face glowed in the subtle light and Noah couldn't stop from reaching out and taking her hand, stroking it with his thumb.

He shifted, placing a knee on the couch between her legs and easing up over her. Keeping his movements slow, he waited for a sign of fear or doubt from her, but the way that pink tongue came out to lick her lips was all the indication he needed. That and the heavy rise and fall of her chest as her breathing quickened.

Reaching for the buttons on his shirt, which she wore so much better than he ever did, he slid one button, then another, then another open until he reached where her sling lay. Her tanned, flat abdomen stared back at him; her belly button held a small blue stone twinkling in the low light.

His hands gripped her waist as he leaned down to kiss her stomach and let his tongue flick the gem. She felt so smooth beneath his lips, he moved lower. Once more he glanced up at her to see her staring back at him, her face flushed, her breathing heavy. How could he not move forward with this?

He might regret it later, but he'd had regrets before. And now he wanted to taste Callie the way he'd been fantasizing about for months. This was nothing more than physical. He wouldn't let it be.

With both hands, he slid his fingers inside the waistband of her shorts and eased them down. He stripped them all the way off and flung them aside. Staring down at her plain pink cotton panties was more of a turn-on than if she were lying here in a red teddy. She was simple, she was real, she was wearing his shirt and for now she was his.

He skimmed a finger across the top band of her panties, then slid his fingers along the elastic that hugged her thighs. She was already hot and wet. For him.

Easing the moist fabric aside, he slid one finger into her heat. Her body arched up as she dug her heels into his couch. Slowly in and out he worked her until she was rocking her hips and gripping the cushion with her good hand.

Perfect. Just how he wanted her.

He dipped his head and slid his tongue over her, pleased when she cried out. He spread her legs farther with his shoulders and kept hold of the panties with one hand while his mouth and other hand continued to assault her.

Her moans, her heavy breathing, her tilted hips against him had him working harder to bring her pleasure.

And he didn't have to wait long. Her body arched, froze and she gasped. Noah stayed right with her until she stopped trembling.

"That was the most erotic thing I've ever seen," he whispered as he let her panties slide back into place.

Her eyes found his and a slight flush crept over her cheeks. "Um…watching a movie isn't what it used to be," she joked.

He put his arm along the back of the couch and leaned toward her face. "You don't have to be embarrassed or uncomfortable."

Her eyes darted to his groin. "Speaking of uncomfortable…"

Noah smiled. "Yeah, it is, but that was all for you. I've been wanting to do that for some time."

Callie tried to ease herself up, but before she had to struggle, Noah offered a hand and pulled her up with her good arm.

"You can't just stay like that," she said, pointing to the obvious. "I want to—"

He placed a fingertip over her lips. "I know you want to, and believe me, so do I. But this isn't the time."

Callie's heavy-lidded eyes darted to the floor as she nodded. Damn, he hadn't meant it that way.

"Hey," he said softly, taking her chin in his hand and forcing her to look at him. "This has nothing to do with you physically. I just think you've been through enough and I hadn't exactly planned on seducing you in my home."

Her eyes studied him. "It's okay, Noah. You're right. This isn't good timing and you obviously have something in your past you're still working through."

He dropped his hand and sat back. "You know nothing about my past, Callie, so you'd best not bring it up again."

She sighed as she sat back against the arm of the sofa. "I was just making an observation. That's all."

Noah cursed and came to his feet, raking a hand through his hair. "No, I'm sorry. There are just some topics that I cannot talk about with anyone, and my past is one of them. I'm still sorting through some rough things, but that's really none of your concern and has no place here."

God, he was such a liar. No place here? Didn't he carry those demons around with him everywhere? Didn't he put them down beside him in bed each night? Hadn't they brought him to Callie and inadvertently led to her accident? How the hell could he say they had no place when in fact they had every place imaginable in his life right now?

He looked back down at her, clad in nothing but his shirt, which was unbuttoned from her rib cage down, exposing those soft panties he'd just been inside.

"I have someone coming to look at the house tomorrow. I'd like to take you out—"

"Noah," she started, but stopped when he held up his hand.

"I know you're not comfortable," he told her. "But I was thinking of just going to the park for a picnic in the shaded area where no one is lingering. Or we could visit my friend Max."

"The movie star?" She laughed. "Yeah, like he wants me in his house."

"Actually, he's called to check on you," Noah told her, turning to face her fully and placing his hands on his hips. "He's one of my best friends, and if you're not comfortable with the picnic, we can hang at his place for a few hours. He won't mind a bit."

"Of course." She tried to button the shirt with only one hand. "This is your house and you're putting your life on hold for me. I'm being a jerk trying to get picky about where I go. Actually, we can go to my place if you want. I could grab some more things and get my mail, check my messages."

Noah nodded as he sat on the edge of the couch and slid her hand aside so he could adjust the buttons.

Why hadn't he thought of her place? Maybe because that was just another level of Callie he was afraid to enter. While she was here, on his turf, he was fine. But if they went to her place, he would be so out of his territory....

"That will be fine," he conceded. "We can pick up some lunch and eat at your apartment. The real-estate agent is coming at noon, so I'd say we need to be gone by eleven-thirty."

"I'll be ready," she informed him. "But, um...are you sure you're okay?"

He cocked his head, and when her eyes darted to his lap, Noah laughed.

"I'm okay," he assured her. "I promise this isn't my first hard-on and it won't be my last where you're concerned."

Nine

Callie was so confused. She wanted to read more into last night's little escapade, but how could she when he'd only been on the giving end and not the receiving?

Had to be out of pity. But what man did that? She'd never known a man to put her sexual needs first. Of course, she hadn't had that many lovers by which to judge.

Mercy, she was beyond confused.

As Noah wove his way through the streets toward her apartment, she was trying to recall if it was clean. Oh, well, too late now, and it wasn't as if she had a cleaning service to come in and take over.

He pulled up in front of her building and came around to help her out.

"My key is in the side pocket of my purse," she told him, holding her bag with her left hand while he dug out the keys.

Noah unlocked her door and ushered her in. "While you

gather more things, I'll get the food from the car and meet you in the kitchen."

Callie nodded and headed to her room. With her right arm snug against her body thanks to the sling, she had to tug on drawers with her left hand, one side at a time until they sprang free.

She grabbed more underwear, because she just couldn't bear to ask Noah to wash hers, a few more shorts and the few button-down shirts she owned. As much as she liked wearing his, she knew she couldn't go on like that the whole time she was with him.

She tossed all that she wanted onto the bright orange comforter and went in search of a tote. She had a slew of tote bags from various pharmaceutical companies when sales reps came into the office.

She found a bag and began putting her items into it and hoisted it up onto her good shoulder with only a slight wince as she pulled too hard and jarred the broken collarbone.

She needed another pain pill, but she was afraid to ask Noah after his reaction the other day.

After placing the bag by the door, she turned to see Noah at her two-seater table spreading out their Chinese food containers.

"Smells great," she told him. "I've been craving Moo Shu Pork for a while."

He smiled and looked up at her. "We just had it in the office two weeks ago."

Callie shrugged. "Then I've been craving it for two weeks. Seems like so much longer. I could eat this stuff every day."

He pulled out their egg rolls and turned toward the kitchen. "What do you want to drink?"

Callie moved past him. "I can get it, Noah. It's my apartment. Let me."

"No, you sit. I can get the drinks."

She sighed. "You're not going to let me win this little argument, either, are you?"

He grinned and that damn head tilted sideways as if he just knew his charm would win any battle he fought.

"Fine. I'll take some ice water. I can't imagine there's much else in there. I was due to go to the store after the photo shoot."

The photo shoot. At least she could say the words now without breaking into a crying fit or turning into a total bear and growling at everyone. Well, not everyone. Just Noah.

"It's no problem. Water is fine with me, too." He came back to the table with two bottles of water and unscrewed hers for her. "Eat up."

"You don't have to tell me twice."

They ate in silence, but something kept digging at her curiosity and she wanted to approach it. Even if he'd told her to back off.

"Why sell the house if you don't really want to?" she asked.

His fork froze at his mouth before he dropped it back into the box. "What makes you think I don't want to sell?"

"Because I've seen your face when you talk about the house being for sale and I saw your face when you told me the real-estate agent was coming by today. You're not happy about this decision, so why make it?"

Noah sighed and eased back in his seat. "Part of me needs to, but the other part of me is afraid to."

Well, that revelation shocked her. Noah Foster afraid of something? She'd seen the sadness and occasional darkness in his eyes, but she'd never believed he'd admit to fear.

"Then why the rush?" Callie asked. "Wait until you're not afraid anymore."

"I have a feeling that fear will never go away. It's just something I need to do."

"Does this have anything to do with that past you don't want to discuss?"

His lips thinned as he eased forward in his seat and grabbed his fork. "Leave it, Callie. You're purposely dancing on shaky ground."

She crossed her legs and sat back in her creaky chair. "So you can pry into my life and make me face my fear, but I can't do the same to you?"

"We don't share the same fears," he told her. "Not even close."

"Really? Why don't you try me?"

"I don't want to try you," he told her, his hands on his hips, his lips thin. "This is not up for debate."

"I don't find it fair that you can dig into my life, my personal space, and then tell me that a part of you isn't up for discussion." She remained in her seat because as much as she wanted to stand up and shout, at least one of them needed to remain calm. "I thought we were moving toward something, Noah."

"We have a sexual attraction, Callie. I'm not looking for more, and honestly, I wasn't even looking for that."

"Okay, no need to be so blunt," she told him, trying to hide the hurt. "I'm just trying to help you. You know, like you're helping me?"

"I'm helping you as a doctor."

Okay, now she did come to her feet. "Really?" she asked, resting her good hand on her hip. "So what happened on your couch last night was, what? You playing doctor?"

"Don't make this into something it's not."

"And what is that? I don't even know what the hell is going on because you're so closed off."

"I have to be closed off," he retorted, his voice booming. "You don't know the pain I went through, the pain I still live with."

"No, I don't because you won't let me. You are always flirty, always eager to make me happy, but you're miserable, Noah. I can see it now that I've spent more time with you."

"You think you know me because you shared a few nights in my house and worked for me for a few months? Because we shared an intimate evening? There's so much, Callie. So much in my heart, in my life, that you don't know."

"Then tell me so I can help," she pleaded. "This can go both ways, you know. Keeping your hurt or anger bottled up can't be healthy."

"Maybe not, but talking about it also makes it…"

"What? Real?"

He closed his eyes and sighed. "I just want it to go away."

"Yeah, I know how you feel." She'd give anything if this living nightmare she was in would vanish. "Please, Noah, let me in."

"You want in?" He opened his eyes, met hers, and she was surprised to find not only anger lurking in those mesmerizing gray eyes but also unshed tears. "Getting in would mean more than I can give right now, Callie. Trust me, you don't want to live my hell."

She tilted her chin and stepped closer. "I don't want to live mine, either, but I am."

Callie's cell chimed through the room, cutting the tension with the upbeat ringtone.

She crossed the room and rummaged with her left hand through her purse. She glanced at the screen and sighed.

"Hi, Amy," she greeted her agent.

"Just calling to check on you. How are you feeling?"

Callie glanced over her shoulder to Noah, who was staring back at her. He could be part of her private life and she couldn't be part of his?

She turned her back and walked to the front window. Her apartment wasn't big, but at least moving away would give off the silent hint that he wasn't welcome to listen to her conversation.

"I'm getting better every day," Callie responded, trying to sound upbeat.

"I just want you to know that the role has been recast for the Anthony Dane movie." Amy paused before lowering her voice. "I'm so sorry, Callie. I didn't want this to happen, but there was nothing we could do. They start shooting next month."

Callie swallowed the burn in her throat and bit her lips to keep from crying. "Um…it's okay. I mean, it's not, but like you said, there's nothing that can be done."

Callie watched as a couple pushed their baby stroller down the street and as a little boy rode by on his bike. Life went on for everyone else while her world had crumbled. She didn't know if she had the strength to build it back up again.

"I'm here," Amy went on. "As long as it takes to get you back to your old self, I'll be here, Callie. I have faith in you."

Callie blinked back the tears. "Thanks. Listen, I need to go. We'll talk later."

Callie ended the call before her emotions exploded. She hated crying on the phone. Who wanted to listen to a blubbering mess on the other end? After sliding the phone into the pocket of her capris, she put her left hand over her eyes and willed the inevitable crying jag away. But it was a moot point because the second she felt Noah's strong hand on her shoulder, she fell back against that hard, sturdy chest and lost it.

He didn't say a word, but he did turn her so she was facing him. She leaned against him, her face against his chest. She was probably going to soak his shirt, but she couldn't stop the tears any more than she could change her fate.

His warm hand roamed up and down her back as he rested his chin on top of her head. Callie knew as soon as she looked up at him she'd see pity, and that was the last thing she wanted. Right now she just needed to get this cry out of her way. Of course, she'd been saying that a lot lately. But she just couldn't help it.

"I knew the part wasn't mine anymore," she whispered against his chest. "But it still hurts to know I've officially lost it."

"There will be others, Callie," he told her softly. "If Anthony Price wanted you once, he'll look at you again."

She eased back and shook her head. "He wanted the flawless Callie. I doubt he'll have use for a scarred Callie. Men can pull off imperfections and Hollywood thinks it's rugged and sexy. A woman has to be regal and flawless at all times to be considered."

Noah nodded. "I won't lie, that's pretty accurate. But I also know you're a fighter and I know I'm a damn good surgeon. Together we won't let this dream of yours disappear."

She studied his face. "I still don't understand why you're so hell-bent on helping me. Yes, I worked for you and I know we shared some…moments, but you're putting your life on hold. Why?"

He reached up and stroked her good cheek. "Because I can't sit back and watch someone I care about suffer. I couldn't live with myself if I didn't try to make your life better."

Callie jerked back. "You care for me?"

Noah stepped forward. "It would be impossible not to feel something more than friendship toward you, Callie. I've tried to ignore the sexual pull, but after tasting you last night, I've been unable to think of little else."

"But just a moment ago you were so adamant about this thing between us being nothing."

Holding her with his mesmerizing gaze, he said, "That's because I wanted to ignore this pull, but when I hold you, I can't lie. My actions betray me."

Shivers raced over Callie's body. "This timing isn't the best, Noah. Especially since you're struggling with...whatever."

"As much as I wish we could explore this, I'm afraid I just can't go into something with you when I don't even know what demons you battle or what my future holds."

He picked up her hand and kissed her knuckles. "Then we'll take this slow. I never back away from what I want, Callie, and I want you. In my bed."

"Well, that was blunt."

"And honest," he told her. "I'm done lying to you, to myself. I guess I'm learning you need to take what you want when you want it because it could be gone in an instant."

She listened to his tone grow almost angry, yet nostalgic.

"Noah, I can't be a replacement for whatever happened to you. You act as if I'm plan B in whatever went wrong in your past. That's not how I want to live. I'll never play second to anything or anyone."

"And you shouldn't have to," he told her, stroking her cheek. "But I want you to know where I stand and why I'm so adamant about being with you again."

Callie leaned into his touch. "I'd be a fool to lie and tell you I haven't thought about you, fantasized about you. But right now the last thing I feel is sexy."

He stepped back and nodded. "You can't help how you feel, but know this. I find you damn sexy, Callie. No matter what you look like on the outside. To me, you're a sexy woman because of your kick-ass attitude and your personality. I know that's unusual for a man to say, but it's true. *Sexy* doesn't have to mean *flawless*."

Callie laughed. "I hope you're not going to use that for your new ad slogan."

The corners of Noah's mouth kicked up. "No, that's for your ears only."

"Then I won't tell anyone," she replied, but her smile faded. "Noah, I know this probably doesn't need to be said, but—"

"No, it doesn't." He cut her off. "I don't want to hear it."

She looked down at her feet, then back up beneath her lashes, afraid to fully look him in the eyes. "I'm sorry I let you down for the new ads."

Noah closed that final sliver of space between them and took hold of her face with both hands, careful of where he touched her right side. "Listen to me and look me straight in the eye. I don't care about the ads. They will go on and something else will work out. Those ads are the last thing I'm worried about right now."

"I realize you're not worried, but your new office is supposed to open in a couple months and you didn't have anything else planned."

"No, I didn't," he agreed, smoothing her hair off her forehead and away from the bandage. "But I also know that something will come to me, and the ad agency I hired is on it. We're looking at a few options, but nothing is final. We may not use a model now. We're looking at something simple with a catchy slogan."

"You're so good to me," she whispered. "Even though I've done nothing but bring you misery, you're amazing. Don't think I'm not grateful. Even when I yell at you and cry, I'm still thankful to have you in my life."

Callie wrapped her arms around his waist and hugged him, because she'd just seen another flash of fear, of angst, spear through his eyes, and she didn't want to get into another argument on whether or not he should open up to her. One day soon, she vowed, she'd get those demons from his closet and then she could help him bury them where they belonged.

Ten

She'd hidden long enough.

Callie hadn't lied when she told Noah that he didn't need to worry about her and to have his normal life with his friends over. This was his house and she was his guest.

But Noah's best friend was the hottest actor in Hollywood and here she looked like Frankenstein's project gone awry.

Callie took a deep breath and smoothed down the simple backless sundress she'd snaked up over her body. But she'd be lying if she tried to pretend she didn't love wearing Noah's soft cotton shirts, because even though they'd been laundered, they still had the very sexy masculine scent of his cologne. And once when he hadn't been looking, she totally turned her nose straight into the collar and took a long, deep inhale.

Just because she was battered and vulnerable didn't mean she didn't still have needs, emotions and a craving for the man.

Callie moved down the wide hallway leading to the patio

doors off the kitchen. Before she stepped outside, she stopped to admire the fine scenery the two men on the patio made. They were opposite in so many ways, yet both of them were so sexy that a woman couldn't help but notice them.

Noah had that dark hair, sultry smile and bedroom eyes. Clichéd as it sounded, the description fit him perfectly. The man always had those heavy lids that screamed *Do me, baby*.

Max, on the other hand, had that messy dark blond hair that never quite seemed fixed but worked for him and his carefree ways. He was quick to smile and always flashed those dimples. He'd starred in so many films recently, Callie would be fooling herself if she didn't admit she was jealous of his string of luck.

No. She was not going to let her thoughts ruin Noah's company or his day. She was a guest. She didn't have to stay out and socialize the whole time, but she did owe it to Noah not to sit inside and pout like a child.

She pushed the door open and stepped out onto the warm stone patio. She hadn't bothered with shoes since she was just going to be by the pool.

"I hope you like your steak still mooing on your plate," Max said with that signature smile. "Noah here likes to barely get them warm before he pulls them off."

"You're just cranky because Abby had to cancel at the last minute and you're dateless." Noah flipped the large hunks of meat and closed the grill lid. "I'll have you know I have had those on there for ten minutes."

Callie smiled. "I'd prefer mine to be dead and not still bleeding."

Max laughed. "Take yours off and leave mine and hers on. I'll man the grill."

Noah turned to his friend, using his tongs as a pointer. "No one mans my grill but this man."

Laughing, Callie moved to the steps of the pool and eased

down onto the top one to put her feet into the refreshing, cool water.

"I'm sorry about the movie, Callie."

She jerked her attention to Max, who was also coming to sit on the top step with her.

"Thank you. It's been…hard to digest."

Max nodded. "I imagine. I can't compare my experience to yours, but I was turned down for a role I wanted once. It was the one role I knew would really launch my career."

Intrigued, Callie shifted to face him better. "Really?"

"I was overlooked because of my height."

Callie knew Noah was taller, but she'd never thought of Max as short by any means.

"Your height?"

"The producer wanted someone well over six foot and I'm just at six even. I didn't figure a few inches would make a difference. Apparently, I was wrong."

Callie extended her legs and swirled them around the water. She hadn't known how Max got started in the industry. He seemed to have just exploded onto the screen.

"Looking back, I'm thrilled I didn't get that role," he went on. "That movie ended up tanking in the box office and the part I would've played was cut out except for a few scenes."

Callie rested her feet back on the smooth step and leaned back onto her good hand. "Wow. I had no idea."

His eyes met hers and Callie could easily see why all the ladies swooned over him.

"Every actor has a story, Callie," he told her with a soft smile. "We don't always jump straight into stardom, and we fight to get where we are. And if Anthony Price wanted you in this film, I can guarantee you he will look at you again."

Callie shook her head. "I'm not so sure."

"I am," he told her with confidence. "I know Anthony and

he's a great guy. They have so many makeup artists and tricks they can pull to make that scar disappear."

If only it were that easy....

"But I'd have to go into a casting call looking like this," she told him. "That's a strike against me."

"Perhaps," he agreed, resting his muscular arms on his legs and leaning forward. "But your acting skills will override any scar. They'll see your talent and know any good makeup artist can fix that."

More hope bloomed within her and she so wanted to believe every word he was saying.

"If you two are done, these steaks are officially dead," Noah called from the other side of the patio.

Max came to his feet, extending his hand to help her up, and smiled. "He gets grouchy when I tell him how to cook."

Callie laughed. "If you hadn't, I would've."

"Fine, then," Noah mocked as he set the platter of meat on the patio table. "Next time you two know-it-alls can make me dinner while I sit by the pool."

Callie shrugged. "Fine with me, but I'm not a good cook, so you're just punishing yourself."

Max laughed: "Yeah, well, I'm an excellent cook. That's how I was raised. My parents own a large chain of restaurants on the East Coast."

"And how are you still single?" she joked, taking a seat.

Max threw her a smile. "I'm having too much fun."

Noah served the steaks and brought out some potato salad and drinks. Callie was thankful for this break in her new daily life of worrying and wondering about her future. Not only was this a great distraction, the uplifting words from Max really made her feel as if something in the future could open up for her. It might not be for a while, not until after Noah performed surgery or whatever he had in mind, but at least there was that proverbial light at the end of the tunnel and it was calling her name.

The following week brought Callie even more happiness. The stitches were out and her first microdermabrasion treatment was over. Callie hoped to God she was on the road to recovery.

She'd stayed at the office because Noah had a few patients to see and Marie had needed to leave early to get her granddaughter to a doctor's appointment. So here she sat in the receptionist's chair like she had so many times before. Only, all those other times she hadn't been so self-conscious.

Marie had simply hugged her and with tear-filled eyes declared how happy she was that Callie was back and looking beautiful. Callie knew the woman was just being kind and Callie didn't correct her about being "back."

Noah was finishing up with the final patient and Callie couldn't wait to get back home, or to Noah's home, where she felt safe, all tucked away from Hollywood's critical eye.

When the phone rang, Callie swiveled around in her cushy chair and picked up the receiver.

"Dr. Foster's office."

"Hello, my name is Mary Harper and my son, Blake, has an appointment next week. I was just calling to see if there were any cancellations before then."

Callie pulled up the screen with the appointments and scanned through. She knew Noah's schedule was pretty tight considering he'd taken off so much and had cut back on his workdays to be home with her, but she looked, anyway.

"I'm sorry, Mrs. Harper, but I don't see any. Is there any way I can take your name and number and we can call you if something opens earlier?"

The lady on the other end sighed. "That would be wonder-

ful. Blake is so anxious to see the doctor. He's afraid to go
back to school until his face and arm are better."

Callie knew this must be the ten-year-old boy Noah spoke
of a couple weeks ago. The little boy who'd been burned.
Noah was doing this appointment as a favor to a client. She
knew he didn't usually take on children or burn victims,
though not because he wasn't capable. Noah was one of the
top surgeons in the country, but he tended to specialize in
breast augmentations, face-lifts and other enhancement pro-
cedures on women.

Callie glanced at the screen again, feeling even guiltier
for keeping Noah from helping this boy who had such high
hopes. Callie understood those hopes.

"Mrs. Harper," Callie said, "could you bring Blake in tomorrow at five?"

"But I thought—"

"I think one more patient at the end of the day won't over-
work Dr. Foster too much, and since this is the consultation,
it won't be a long appointment."

Mrs. Harper burst into tears and instantly Callie teared
up. "You don't know what this means to us," the woman
said. "Truly. You don't know how thankful I am you can fit
him in sooner. I just want my son to have a little hope. We'll
be there."

Once Callie hung up, she added the last appointment. If she
had to come to the office herself and stay by Noah's side then
she would. There was no way she could sit in Noah's lavish
home being babysat by the doctor when he was needed here
so much more. There was a boy afraid to go to school, afraid
to see his friends, all because he was imperfect.

The irony was not lost on her and she prayed the young
boy would find the courage to go back to school, even if his
scars couldn't be healed.

When the last patient came out, Callie was all ready to

take her chart and file it. Thankfully, the woman didn't have a co-pay, so she breezed right on out the door. When the busty blonde had checked in, Callie had had her head down looking at another chart, so she'd bypassed the whole awkward situation of seeing beauty staring her in the face.

God, she didn't know how long she could continue to work here. There was no way she could dodge all the beauty that came in and out the door.

Once the client was gone, Callie locked the front door and set the alarm for the front of the building. After turning off the lights for the waiting room and shutting down the computer, she went to Noah's office.

"You ready to go?" he asked her as he shut down his own computer.

Callie nodded. "Yeah."

He glanced up at her, his brows drawn. "Something wrong?"

"I just got off the phone with Mrs. Harper. Blake will be here tomorrow at five."

Noah shook his head. "His appointment is next week. I'll be home with you tomorrow afternoon."

Callie crossed her arms over her chest. "No. Tomorrow at five you and I will both be here. If you can't leave me at home to take care of myself, I will come with you. He needs to be seen. Needs to know that there's hope for him."

Noah crossed the room and stood within inches of her, making her tilt her head to meet his eyes.

"Of course there's hope," Noah told her, cupping her cheek. "I plan to do everything I can for him. I can't imagine how he must feel. He's been away from school for so long, first because he needed to stay away in case of infection and now because he feels he would get made fun of. His feelings must be all over the place."

Callie nodded. "I know they are," she whispered.

Noah stroked her smooth, unmarred cheek and laid a gentle kiss on her lips. "You're amazing, Callie."

"Why?"

"To stay here, to come back tomorrow in order to help a young boy. You just amaze me over and over."

Callie shook her head. "Noah, if I can help this one boy have something to cling to, something that will give him the inspiration to believe that he's the same kid with or without the burns, then my staying here is totally worth it."

"He's the same kid, huh?" Noah asked with a slight grin. "Sound like something I told you before?"

Callie shook her head. "This is a kid, Noah. I'm not the same person now. Something changed in me, something I'm not sure I'll ever get back."

Her heart clenched when he pulled her against him, careful of her shoulder, and lightly touched his lips to hers.

"You'll get it back," he murmured against her mouth. "We'll get it back."

How could she not cling to his strength, his faith? How could she give up when Noah was giving all he had for her?

Callie knew that if a little boy had faith, and Noah had this grand amount of confidence, she should feel the same. Fate might have taken her off her path, but she was on a new path now, and the decisions she made would alter the next course she took.

Callie waited in Noah's office while he had the consultation the following day with Blake. She didn't want to see the young boy, didn't want to be reminded that people had worse problems than her. She knew that. She even felt guilty for her self-induced pity parties. But she just couldn't see Blake, though she was eager to hear Noah's prognosis.

Thankfully, Marie was heading up the reception desk and Callie could hide back here. She didn't want to be out front again for a while, though now that her stitches were out and the bandage off, she didn't feel as much like Frankenstein, but she still had a sling and a long, red scar on her face.

Callie glanced at the clock and wondered what her parents were doing. She hadn't told them about the accident. She still didn't want to, but they were her parents and she'd always prided herself on her honesty.

She pulled her cell from her pocket and resigned herself to the fact she'd probably be having one of the most depressing phone conversations ever.

Her parents' phone rang and she tightened her grip on her cell.

"Hello."

"Mom?"

"Callie? Darling, it's so good to hear from you."

Her mother's smile sounded in her tone and Callie could picture the woman standing by the stove cooking, as she often did.

"I didn't expect to catch you home, Mom. Are you not working today?"

Erma Matthews sighed. "Well, they had to cut my hours back at the grocery, so I'm only doing single shifts now."

Callie closed her eyes, rubbed her temple and eased back in Noah's cushy leather office chair. "I'm so sorry, Mom. I assume since the phone is back on you got the money from the account."

"Yes, honey. Thank you. I just hate you're spending your hard-earned money on us. Hopefully, your father will find something soon. He's actually got a job interview in two days at a factory about an hour away. It would be a commute, but the pay is even better than what he was making before the layoff."

A sliver of hope slid through her. "That's wonderful, Mom."

For a moment, silence entered their conversation. Callie toyed with the dark buttons on the brown leather chair, knowing she was going to have to come clean.

"Mom, I need to tell you something and I don't want you to worry."

"What's wrong? Are you all right? You can't tell a mother not to worry and expect her not to, Callie."

Callie swallowed and eased forward in the chair, resting her elbow on the desk while holding the phone to her ear on her uninjured side.

"I was in an accident a couple weeks ago. But I'm fine," she quickly added. "I have a broken collarbone and I had some stitches, but I'm fine."

"Good heavens, honey. Why didn't you text your brother and have him tell us?"

Shame. Humiliation. Risk of sounding like a failure.

"I didn't want you all to worry. But because of the timing of the accident, I won't be able to fulfill my role in the Anthony Price movie I told you about."

"Oh, honey." Erma's tone softened and Callie imagined that tilt of the head most mothers got when they felt a twinge of regret. "I'm so sorry, sweetheart. I know how much you wanted that."

Wanted? No. She craved it, ached for it.

"There will be other roles," her mother assured her. "What's meant to be is what will happen."

"Listen, Mom," Callie said, trying to hold back tears, "I'm at the office and I need to go. I just wanted to touch base and let you know what was going on."

"I'm so glad you called. I love you so much."

"Love you, too, Mom."

Callie disconnected the call, calling herself all kinds of coward for not disclosing the full extent of her injuries. But she just couldn't. She'd left her mother with the hope that there would be more roles, more movies. But the reality was there probably wouldn't be.

A moment later, Noah stepped into the office and hung his lab coat on the back of his door. Without a word he moved to the desk, opened the side drawer and pulled out his keys.

"I'm ready."

Callie watched as he walked out the door and turned to head out the back way.

Um…okay. Apparently, something was wrong, but since he was already walking away, she couldn't ask.

She nearly chased him out the back door and into his car, which he had already started. After getting in and barely having time to put on her seat belt, she glanced over.

"I assume Marie will lock up?"

Noah nodded and maneuvered into traffic.

"Would you like to tell me what happened to make you so upset?"

"No."

He didn't look at her, didn't elaborate, simply drove toward his home. Callie knew when to keep her mouth shut, though she hated that he was obviously at war with himself and it didn't take a genius to figure out it more than likely had something to do with the young boy he'd just had a consultation with.

Callie only prayed that the boy and his mother hadn't left on the same upsetting note that Noah had.

By the time they pulled into his garage, the tension was thick and Callie thought it best if she just went into the house. If he wanted to talk, he would. Though she wasn't counting on it. He was closed off when it came to anything personal.

Before she could grip her door handle, he turned off the ignition and slammed his palm onto the steering wheel with a loud thump.

"Damn it."

Callie sat still, waiting to see if he was going to open up and vent.

"I don't know if I can do this, Callie." Noah stared straight ahead to the white garage wall. "I can't work on that little boy and not get attached."

Callie bit her lip, not wanting to interrupt.

"He sat there looking at me with all that hope in his eyes and I want to deliver on promises his mother has made to make him well again. I want to be the hero he seems to think I am."

Callie reached over, touched his arm. "Then what's stopping you?" she asked.

"What if I fail?"

Noah turned, meeting her gaze. And there was that pain she'd seen a glimpse of before. Now it was raw, no longer hiding, and he wasn't trying to keep it under control.

"I refuse to fail another person, Callie."

Another person? Who had he failed before?

"Noah—"

He got out of the car and went into the house, slamming the door as he went. Callie sighed and rested her head against the leather seat. The man was going to break. If he didn't open up soon, he was going to shatter, and then all of his secrets, all of his feelings, were going to be laid open for all to see and there would be nothing he could do about it. She prayed that he'd let her help, but he was too stubborn, too strong-willed.

Ironically, some of those qualities that annoyed her she could relate to all too easily.

Eleven

Over a week had passed since the showing of his home and Noah still couldn't call his real-estate agent back with an answer. Yes, the amount the newlyweds had offered was very close to the asking price and higher than any other offers, but he just couldn't bring himself to make that call and get the ball rolling.

Added to that, he'd talked with colleagues about Blake's case and met with the little boy and he was certain he was the best one for the job. But the thought of being the one that little guy pinned his hope on was almost more than Noah thought he could bear. He was still dealing with Callie and all that hero worship she had in her eyes when he discussed her healing process. Both Callie and Blake were looking for something within Noah that he just didn't know if he could give.

For right now, though, he needed to take a step back from being a doctor. He needed to get back to being Callie's friend and letting his workload ease from his mind for just a bit. And he knew just the thing to get them back on friendly footing. He'd had something delivered earlier today and he couldn't wait to show Callie.

She'd laid back down for a nap just after lunch when she'd taken a pain pill. She hadn't had one in a while, but he knew she'd been in pain. She'd been trying to work on her arm exercises even when he'd told her to take it slow.

That pain medication always made her so tired and Noah encouraged her to sleep because resting would help her body heal faster, as well.

She'd taken her sling off today and had promised to go easy on her arm, but he would be keeping a close eye on her. He'd done the microdermabrasion last week and he was hoping to do more next week. If he could work on her wound as often as medically possible, perhaps her healing time would lessen and her scar would not be so visible.

It was so hard to shut down his doctor mind-set. Right now, though, he had something else in mind. Something fun.

He wanted to show Callie her surprise, but she was still asleep. He walked into the kitchen and saw the painkiller bottle on the counter. A sick feeling overcame him. For so long he'd lived with bottles floating around...usually empty ones that had just been prescribed only days before.

But this sick feeling didn't stem from his past; it came from the fact that Noah knew he hadn't left the bottle out when he'd given her a pill earlier that morning. He glanced at the clock on the stove and knew it was just now time for another pill, so why was this bottle out?

He twisted the cap off and counted the pills. It was two short compared to what should've been in there.

She'd taken that extra one the other day, which meant she'd taken another one today At this point, she shouldn't be taking two pills in the same day. Her pain had to have significantly lightened, so she should be able to get by with just an over-the-counter medication.

He'd thought he could leave them out and not treat her like a child. Apparently, he was wrong.

Not taking any more chances, Noah put the lid back in place and gripped the bottle as he set off for her bedroom. By the time he reached the second floor, he was angry, upset and feeling a little betrayed. If she was lying to him, he wasn't going to help her anymore. He couldn't live like that again. Not to mention the fact he couldn't be her doctor if she wouldn't follow orders.

He eased the door open and saw her lying on her side, her hands tucked beneath her uninjured cheek. The covers had been kicked off and she'd opened her window to let the afternoon breeze blow in. Crimson strands danced around her shoulders and her breathing was slow, soft.

Moving into the room, he placed the bottle on the nightstand and eased down onto the edge of her bed. The movement caused her to stir and soon her lids fluttered open until she focused on him. She looked like she had the other night, just before he'd made love to her with his mouth. So much for putting distance between them.

"Did you take a pill without telling me?" he asked, not even trying to hide his irritation.

She blinked, eased up onto her side and looked him in the eye. "I took one just before I lay down. I think I overdid it with taking my sling off. I only did a few more exercises than usual with my arm, but it started hurting more than it had been."

He picked up the bottle, marched into her adjoining bathroom and flushed the pills. When he came back out she was on her feet and angry.

"Why did you do that?" she cried.

"Because I'm afraid you'll get hooked. These are highly addictive. And I told you if you did that again I'd flush them."

Callie laughed. "I won't get addicted, Noah. I took a pill only a little before it was due. I'd had the other one in my system for over six hours. It's not like I was going to OD."

Even the term made him ill. The image of how he'd found Malinda was embedded in his head for the rest of his life. He found himself instantly seeing Callie that way and the thought made him want to vomit.

"If you're going to stay in my house and allow me to be your doctor, you will do exactly what I say, when I say it, or I won't help you anymore. I thought we'd already settled this."

Callie stepped back, blinking. "Wow. Um…okay. Calm down. I promise not to do anything else without asking."

He stared at her for several seconds. He needed to get a grip.

What he really needed to do was remember this wasn't Malinda and he truly didn't believe Callie had a drug problem. He needed to lighten up before he drove her away. Then what good would he be to her?

God, his past had consumed him and overtaken his emotions, fueling his anger. Callie still had nearly a whole bottle of pills, and if this were Malinda, that bottle would've been gone within a few days. Callie had been here a few weeks.

He took a deep breath, trying to erase the previous images of fighting with Malinda.

Remembering the surprise, he told her, "I had something delivered and I was hoping you'd be awake when it came, but you slept through it all."

She tilted her head and grinned. And just like that she'd forgiven him for bursting in and yelling at her. Yeah, she was quite different from Malinda.

"What is it?" she asked, smile beaming. "Did you get a dog? I've always wanted a dog like the one I left back in Kansas."

He laughed. "Um, no dog. This is something else you left back in Kansas."

Her brows drew together and she shook her head. "My old beat-up Jeep with the broken horn and busted grill?"

Taking her hand, he pulled her toward the door. "Just follow me and stop guessing. You're taking the fun out of the moment."

She shuffled her bare feet along behind him as he led her down the stairs and through the wide hallway toward the back of the house where he had a game room.

When he entered the room, he flicked the light on and stepped aside so she could see.

"Oh, my God," she squealed. "Noah, you didn't!"

Seeing her reaction was so worth paying extra to have the pool table delivered and set up so quickly. "I'm a fan myself and had thought of adding one to the game room, so when you mentioned it, I knew I needed to get one. Max and I used to play in college."

She stood staring and he almost felt a fool at her silence, so he kept rambling.

"Of course, we played while killing a case of beer and talking about women."

Her eyes darted to his and she smiled. "It's nice you two are still so close."

"He's like family," he told her.

She moved farther into the room and ran her hand along the green felt of the pool table. "It's going to be hard to do this with one bad arm."

Stepping closer to her, he grinned and rested a hip on the table beside where her delicate hand roamed. "That's what I'm here for, isn't it? To assist you with things you can't do?"

Her body visibly shivered and he was glad he had that effect on her, because she sure as hell had some amazing sort of power over him.

"Are we going to play now?" she asked, her voice husky.

Noah knew an opportunity when he saw one. Even though he knew in his mind he needed to be her doctor and friend above all else, his libido wasn't receiving that memo. Damn, he wanted her. She was still all rumpled from sleep with her dark crimson hair tumbling around her shoulders, her face free of makeup and the oversize shirt of his hanging nearly off one slender shoulder. He knew beneath that well-worn cotton she wore no bra, because since that first day with her bath, she hadn't asked him to put one on her. She wore these tiny little denim shorts with the frayed edging flirting with her bare thighs.

He assumed she'd managed the zipper and button them without his assistance.

"Yeah," he told her, keeping his gaze on her lips. "We're going to play now."

Callie started to ease forward, but Noah stepped back and cleared his throat. "I'll get a stick."

God, could there be more metaphors between sex and a game of pool? He'd never been turned on playing before. Then again, he'd been playing with Max or other guys from college and they were too busy trash-talking and comparing their previous dates.

Callie maneuvered the balls into the triangle while he chalked up the tip of the stick. "I'll stand behind you," he told her.

She stayed against the table and smiled. "I'll have to push with my left arm, if you can reach around and hold it with your right."

"Gladly."

He was torturing himself. Actually, he'd been torturing himself since he'd completely overstepped his patient/doctor bounds on his sofa the other evening, but that was uncontrol-lable and he'd gotten swept into the moment.

He slid the stick between her waist and her left arm. She grabbed the back of it and shifted her body. Noah wrapped his right arm around her and was careful not to touch her shoulder.

His face was mere inches from her mass of subtle curls. Inhaling, he pulled in a tropical, fruity scent that always seemed to surround Callie, filling his home with her signature intoxicating scent. He eased a bit closer until his mouth was at her ear, her hair tickling his lips.

"Lean into it," he whispered as he eased her body down his own.

Her body bent at the waist and Noah went with her. Together they leaned over the table and he eyed the cue ball.

"Relax," he whispered. "You're breathing hard. Take your time. Focus on what you want to happen."

Damn. If he didn't keep his mouth shut he was going to start pitching a tent in his jeans, and wood behind a zipper was never comfortable or concealable.

"I've done this before, you know." She tilted her head to look at him over her shoulder, but when she did, her mouth brushed against his jaw and he had to steel himself not to turn and take advantage of her lips.

"But it's been a while," he reminded her. "I'm just here to help you remember how everything works."

"Oh, I think I remember," she said with a sultry smile.

Noah swallowed. She was good at this, the flirting and sassy talk she'd done before her accident. She was slowly coming around to her old self.

"Hold the stick firmly," he told her, holding his left hand over hers on the stick. "Don't rush it. Practice stroking it and not letting it go too early."

For pity's sake, shut up, Noah. Why was he using a game of pool as a pathetic form of foreplay? If he wanted her so badly, why was he making himself miserable by holding back? He'd already admitted to her that he wanted her in his bed. There was no going back on that. Sex was simple. It was all that other emotional garbage he couldn't and wouldn't deal with or allow himself to get wrapped up in.

"I got it," she told him and pushed the stick forward until it hit the cue ball into the other balls, sending the various colors rolling around the table.

Two stripes sunk instantly.

"Good job," he told her as he stood up. And yup, there was that pressure against his zipper. *Well done, Noah. Well done. Way to avoid getting an erection.*

"If you thought that was good, you're going to be really impressed," she told him as she rounded the table. "In fact, I think I can take you without your help and using only one arm."

Impressed and intrigued, he crossed his arms and smiled. "Then let's see it, hotshot."

She proceeded to show him just how amazing she was at this game and he was damn glad his friends weren't here to see it. Max would give him hell for losing so easily.

By the time the game was coming to a close and she was ready to sink the eight ball, Noah had had more than enough of seeing her bent over the table wearing those little shorts and his shirt. In the two weeks she'd been at his house, he never got tired of seeing her wearing his shirt. He loved the way it hung on her, occasionally giving him a glimpse of a swell of her breast or the curve of her slender shoulder.

Before she could sink that last ball and totally embarrass him, he snagged an arm around her waist and pulled the stick from her hands. "I think you've shown off enough."

Her gasp of surprise quickly turned into a wide grin. "Sore loser, Noah? I'm not surprised. You're very competitive, but I hate to break it to you. I own this game."

He laid the stick across the end of the table and used both

hands to span her narrow waist. "Yeah, well, there's something else I'd rather own right now."

That smile of hers faltered as she bit her lower lip a second before licking them. Her hand came up to his shoulder, slid around his neck and toyed with the ends of his hair on the nape of his neck.

"I'd swear you planned this, but you had no idea I was getting this table."

Her brows drew together. "Planned what?"

"Those shorts," he told her. "Bending over the edge of the table to take your shots and throwing your rear in my face at every opportunity."

"I certainly had no clue you'd be getting this," she defended. "Besides, it was you who practically dragged me out of bed."

Noah inched closer, pulling her lower body taut against his. "I should've kept you there."

His mouth slammed down onto hers and she responded in an instant. Her body arched against his and he palmed her lower back while his other hand slid up to thread his fingers through her hair.

Her tongue invaded his mouth and Noah nearly sank to his knees. This woman knew how to take as much as he was willing to give. With one arm banded around her waist, he hoisted her up onto the edge of the pool table and stood between her legs. He pulled her forward a tad to stay as close to him as possible. He wasn't about to let her get away, not when he'd been denying himself for so long.

Keeping his mouth locked on hers, he reached between them and slowly unbuttoned each of the buttons, one agonizing hole at a time.

She pulled her mouth from his. "Pull the darn thing."

Noah laughed. "It's my shirt."

"Buy a new one."

"As you wish."

He gave a yank and the last of the buttons scattered across the hardwood floor. Easing the shirt off her shoulders, Noah kept his gaze on her chest. He was a guy—where else was he supposed to look?

"You're magnificent," he whispered. "Don't look away, Callie."

She shook her head. "I'm not. I just… It's hard to have you look at me like this. I mean, you create beauty for a living and I'm just…me. Flawed, but even before nothing special."

He took her face in his hands and kissed her softly before pulling back. "Listen to me. I'm sure as hell not comparing you to anyone. I want you, Callie. You. Because I'm attracted to you. It's that simple."

She reached with her left hand and palmed his cheek. "Then don't let me complicate things with talking, because I'm about to explode."

As if he needed any more of an invitation. He peeled his shirt off and flung it to the side and quickly pulled off his jeans and boxers—but not before grabbing a condom from his pocket and tossing it onto the table.

Callie's eyes widened and he couldn't help but laugh.

"I'm optimistic," he defended with a grin.

"I'm glad, but I'm more shocked at you," she told him, her face turning a cute shade of pink. "It's just…wow. If I were you I'd totally walk around naked and stare at myself."

Noah kissed her. "Shut up, Callie. Let me show you what else we can be doing."

He unfastened her shorts, and with her help of rocking from side to side, he eased them along with her panties down her toned legs before dropping them to the floor.

Noah stepped back to look at her, and even though he knew she was uncomfortable, he wanted her to get comfortable with the fact he enjoyed looking at her.

* * *

Callie wished he'd do something. The way he kept looking at her was making her nervous. He might say he wasn't comparing her to patients, and that was probably true, but he had to at least be comparing her to his past girlfriends, who were no doubt model-perfect.

"Noah?"

"I just wanted to see you. All of you."

He stepped forward again and wrapped his hands around her waist, helping her to ease forward on the table. One hand slid between them to her heat and Callie spread her legs wider. When he parted her, stroked her, she felt unable to stay upright anymore, and she leaned back on her good hand to expose herself more to him.

"That's it," he whispered. "Relax."

He lifted her feet one at a time to rest on the edge of the pool table as he continued to stroke her. When she was splayed before him, he slid one finger inside and started to move slowly in and out. Her hips lifted, needing more, silently begging for more.

"Slow down," he told her. "We've got time."

She looked up at him and saw that he was smiling. He was enjoying her torture. But she wasn't going to beg. He'd like that too much.

She lay back all the way on the table and closed her eyes. Let him take his time with her. She wasn't about to complain.

The sound of the condom wrapper filled the room and she waited with eager anticipation.

With his hands on either side of her inner thighs, he eased her open even more, and she braced herself as he slid into her.

She reached her left arm up and he grabbed it, pulling her back up so her torso met his, causing him to sink fully into her. Her hard nipples rubbed against his coarse hair, his hard chest, and she groaned as he started moving within her.

His hand remained on the small of her back, guiding her body against his, keeping it where they both wanted it.

His other hand clutched the nape of her neck as his mouth captured hers again. His tongue swept through her mouth, mimicking the actions of their bodies. Callie had never felt so much of a man from her head to her toes and all delicious points in between the way she felt Noah.

His breathing quickened as did his rhythm. Callie clutched his shoulder as she kept her body flush against his. His lips left her mouth, but he rested his forehead against hers. Eyes shut, jaw muscle ticking, Noah groaned.

Knowing she could bring him to the point where he looked as if he'd burst was all the initiative she needed to let go. Her body clenched around his as her ankles locked behind his back, her knees digging into his sides.

Noah's head tilted back as his body slammed into hers one last time and then froze as he released. She held him until they stopped trembling, until her body had chilled and he eased back.

With a wry grin, he brushed the hair away from her face. "This was the best addition to my house I think I've ever added."

Twelve

Noah walked down the hallway of the assisted-living facility toward Thelma's room. Her door was slightly ajar and he eased it all the way open to find her sitting in her favorite recliner, asleep. Her color wasn't too good today and it wasn't the first time he'd noticed she was looking more run-down.

As a doctor, he knew she probably didn't have much time, but as the one person who was the closest thing she had to family, the thought seeped into his heart and left a gap that he feared might never close. This was just another piece of Malinda he couldn't hang on to. Not that he wanted to hang on to those nightmare memories, but he wanted desperately to cling to the good times, the dreams they'd shared before drugs murdered their life together.

Noah eased into the room and closed the door. The slight click of the knob had Thelma stirring. She looked up at him and smiled.

"I didn't know I was going to have such a handsome visitor today. What's your name, honey?"

He laughed. Apparently, she wasn't lucid today, but he found it kind of cute at her age she still had that flirty spunk left in her.

"It's Noah, Thelma." He took a seat in the small wooden armchair next to hers. "You remember me. I'm engaged to Malinda. Your granddaughter."

She studied his face for a moment and he didn't think she'd register the names, but finally a slow smile spread across her wrinkly face. "Oh, my beautiful Malinda. Why isn't she here? Is she working?"

"No, she couldn't make it today."

Thelma's smile held. "Well, can you tell her to stop by? I miss seeing her. She's all I have left of my own daughter."

Noah knew Malinda's mother had been gone several years before he'd met Malinda, and Noah hated that Thelma was struggling with that pain all over again. Every time her memory was jogged, she had to relive losing her daughter all over again. There was no way he could tell her about Malinda. He'd let the woman go on believing.

"I'll see what we can do," he assured her. "But I want to know how you're feeling."

Thelma shrugged. "I'm okay. Um…could you call Malinda? I'd really like to talk to her."

That was a first. Usually he could dodge the question of bringing her in, and she'd never asked him to call her.

"She's busy today," he lied. "I promise she misses you, too."

Thelma nodded and grabbed his hand between her frail ones. "She's such a sweet girl. And to be engaged? I bet she's so happy. I can't wait for the wedding. I know my Malinda. She'll be a beautiful bride."

Noah swallowed the lump that crept up with the image.

Yeah, she would've been a beautiful bride. A beautiful wife. Had she stayed clean.

"She always played dress-up when she was little," Thelma went on. "She wanted to be an actress and she would dress up in different costumes and show off. Most of the time she played a bride and would come down the stairs with a pillowcase on her head as her veil."

Noah could easily picture a young Malinda playing dress-up. Acting had been her thing for as long as he'd known her. And eventually that was what killed her.

And he was shocked to realize that for the first time since he'd been coming here alone, the memories didn't hurt nearly as badly. He knew Callie coming into his life was easing that hurt, that guilt. Little by little, Callie was making his life better.

"Did you eat breakfast today?" he asked her, silently pleading for her to dodge the topic.

She pursed her lips and let his hand ease away from hers. "Hmm…I'm sure I did, but I can't recall what it was. Fruit, maybe?"

Because so many patients with Alzheimer's forgot to eat, he wanted to make sure she was getting enough calories. "How about if I get you some juice and yogurt?"

"I don't think I have any," she told him.

He moved to her small fridge in the kitchenette and opened it. "I brought a few things over the other day. You have yogurt or cheese and crackers. What would you like?"

"The yogurt, please."

He put it on the small tray and set it on her lap, then went back to get her some juice. He'd wait until she ate and drank it all. He knew it wasn't much, but it was something and he'd been asking the staff to watch her at meals to make sure at least half her plate was clean.

Even as she ate her yogurt, she kept bringing up Malinda. Noah merely nodded and smiled.

But it was so hard to picture Malinda, not because she'd been gone a little over a year, but because when he imagined anyone, it was Callie whose image appeared in his mind.

Guilt slid through him. Did that mean she was replacing Malinda? Could he truly be that heartless? Or was his mind telling him to finally move on, to let go of something, someone who would never be his?

Every time he thought of Callie, the same erotic visual flooded his mind from last night. Callie leaning over his new pool table. Callie spread out on the pool table. Callie wrapped around him on the pool table. He hadn't wanted to let her go when she'd gone up to bed alone.

God, he honestly hadn't meant to cross the line from doctor to man with her, but there was nothing he could've done to stop it. He'd seen the inevitable coming and had warned her, and himself, what to expect, but he'd never expected their uniting to be so powerful, so…memorable. So, yeah, apparently he was replacing Malinda, but not in his heart. He didn't even know if there would ever be room for another woman to fill that gaping hole.

But Callie's warmth and sweet spirit, which was slowly easing back, made him think things he probably shouldn't. And he'd gotten so used to her being in his home, always there when he thought of her. He could admit to himself how much he enjoyed her company on a personal level…sex aside.

Thelma laughed and brought his attention back.

"What?" he asked.

"You have the most peaceful smile on your face," she told him. "I've seen that look. You're in love."

Noah started to deny it, but Thelma assumed he'd been thinking about Malinda—the woman he had been completely in love with.

He just laughed instead of commenting. What could he say that wouldn't be a bald-faced lie?

"I remember when I fell in love with my William." She took a sip of her juice and grinned. "He was the most handsome man ever. Almost as handsome as you."

"Thanks."

"My granddaughter has good taste," she told him. "We don't pick out the ugly ones, but we definitely make sure they're gentlemen, too. I know you're going to treat my Malinda right, like a good husband. Caring for her and providing for her, that's what she needs. She's vulnerable at times, but you're a strong man. I'm so happy she found you."

Noah came to his feet. He couldn't sit here any longer and listen to her go on and on about what a good provider and caring man he was. He wasn't any of those things or Malinda would still be alive.

"Thelma, I have a meeting and need to be going, but I promise to come back tomorrow." He took her tray and set it in the kitchenette. "Is there anything else you need before I go?"

She smiled up at him and shook her head. "Just make sure to bring my Malinda by and tell her I love her."

Noah nodded, kissed her on the cheek and left. Good God. He couldn't keep doing this. How did he release this guilt of letting down not only Malinda, but Thelma? He was a fake, sitting in there smiling, laughing with his dead fiancée's grandmother.

He was a doctor, a profession known for healing people, but right now he felt like a complete failure. And he'd failed the one woman who loved him. He refused to fail Callie, too.

Callie slid her cell back into the pocket of her shorts and resisted the urge to throw something or just break down and cry. When she'd called her mother to see how her parents were,

Callie knew something was wrong. After getting her father on the phone, he claimed a storm had come through and torn off a piece of their roof. He'd put a tarp over it and was hoping to be able to at least patch just that part even though they couldn't afford to do the entire house just yet.

Life was fickle. Either everything was puppy dogs and rainbows or blow after blow kept knocking you down.

On a sigh, she walked down the hall of Noah's house toward the workout room. It had been a while since she'd been on the treadmill because she'd been so afraid to jar her shoulder. But if she just put the setting on a fast walk, she wouldn't be bouncing so much, and honestly, it wasn't hurting at all today. Besides, she really needed that stress reliever so she could clear her mind.

She assumed Noah wouldn't mind if she used this room. He'd never said otherwise.

Callie entered the gym and smiled. The man had thousands of dollars of equipment in here and all she'd ever seen him use was the heavy bag in the corner. She moved to the bag and used her left hand to give it a bit of a shove. Yeah, no wonder they were called heavy bags. And no wonder Noah's arms looked so, so fine. They'd felt pretty fine, too, beneath her fingertips as she'd gripped them while—

She closed her eyes and sighed. What was she doing? Seriously. She was living in her boss's home, letting him care for her, getting intimate with him all the while knowing he wouldn't commit to her beyond the present. He'd said as much, and to be honest, she didn't want to be with someone in a committed relationship when they were holding so many secrets inside. Secrets that were obviously still very painful. So painful he couldn't even mention them.

Or maybe that was the problem. Maybe he just didn't want to mention them to her.

"You look like I feel."

Callie jerked her head up and looked in the mirror-lined wall to see Noah's reflection as he stood in the open doorway. He looked ready for a workout with his running shoes, knit shorts and no shirt. The tattoo of a dragon slid over his shoulder and down onto one pec. He only had one tattoo, but that piece of art really showcased some nice, well-toned muscles.

"Bad day?" she asked, still looking at him in the mirror since he remained in place.

He nodded. "I just got back from the assisted-living facility."

"You go nearly every day. I never wanted to pry, but…do you have a family member there?"

"You could say that. We're not blood related, but I'm all she has."

A piece of Callie's heart melted. Did the man have any flaws?

"Is she worse?" Callie asked. "Sorry, not my business. You just look…worried."

He ran his hands over his face and sighed as he moved into the room. "She's got Alzheimer's and some days are worse than others. She keeps wanting to see her granddaughter."

"What's wrong with that?"

Noah rested his hands on his hips. "Her granddaughter passed away a little over a year ago."

"Oh, God. That's terrible. What happened?"

Noah glanced to the floor and shook his head. "A senseless accident that should've been prevented."

Alarm bells went off in her head. Was this "accident" the cause of the nightmare that plagued his life?

"Can you avoid the topic with her?" Callie asked.

"I've tried. Every time I visit, I dodge it, but that's the one thing she's noticed is missing from her life. Of all the things she's forgotten, she's never forgotten Malinda."

"Families have strong bonds," she murmured. "Some stronger than others."

Noah tipped his head. "Everything okay back home?"

She wasn't ashamed of her background, but she'd never really gotten into the whole situation about how her father lost his job and her mother had to take on an extra one. There was no need to pull out the "I was a poor kid" card. She didn't want pity from anyone. For any reason.

"Not really," she told him honestly. "I may have to go home for a few days."

His brows drew in. "What's wrong?"

Callie shrugged, not wanting to get into too many details because she'd bet every dollar left in her checking account that he'd never had to worry about his electricity or water getting shut off.

"Just some issues I need to deal with and I can't do it from here. Not sure what I can do while I'm there, but I just can't ignore my parents when they need help."

Noah crossed the room and held her gaze in the mirror. "Is there anything I can do?"

"No, but thanks."

He studied her as if he knew she was hiding something. "I can come with you. I'm not sure what's going on, but I'd like to help."

Okay, she'd known he was very generous, very caring, but to offer to fly to Kansas to help people he didn't know with a situation he knew nothing about? God, he really was the proverbial knight in shining armor.

But the last thing she wanted was for him to see where she grew up, because it was the polar opposite of this cushy twelve-thousand-square-foot home.

"You don't need to come," she told him. "You have work and you've taken off enough time to be with me."

"And a few more days won't matter."

She smiled. "Really. I'll be fine and I'll only be gone a couple days. You won't even miss me."

He looked as if he wanted to argue, but then he glanced down to her shoulder.

"How's the collarbone?" he asked.

Apparently, he was very good at reading women and knew when not to start an argument, but she had no doubt he'd get back on the topic of her home life soon…just as she would circle back to his issues, as well.

She lifted her arm until she felt pain. "Feeling much better. It's healing quicker than I thought it would."

"That's because the more it's immobilized, the quicker it can heal. Plus, you're still young and fit. That always helps."

"Maybe being cared for by the best doctor in town helps, too," she told him with a smile.

He returned her grin and stepped forward, coming up directly behind her. "Are you flirting with me?" he asked.

Callie smoothed her hair back from her forehead and shrugged. "What if I was?"

Sliding an arm around her waist and pulling her back against his hard body, Noah leaned down to her ear, all the while keeping his eyes locked on hers in the mirror.

"Then I'd have to do something about that," he whispered. "Are you looking for something beyond flirting?"

Warmth spread through her body at his words, his presence. "Maybe we've both had a bad day. It's never too late to turn it around."

His hand spread across her flat abdomen; his pinkie finger dipped into the waistband of her shorts. "I'm all for making your day better."

He snaked his hand up her shirt, his fingertips grazing the bottom of her breast and sending shivers through her. "Are you sure you can handle everything? I have a feeling this could take a while."

Callie dropped her head back to his shoulder and groaned as his finger and thumb found her nipple. "I'm sure," she murmured, unable to really think, let alone form more than a two-word sentence.

Before he could make good on his promise to improve her day, the doorbell rang.

Noah froze and cursed in her ear. "I'll kill whoever is at the door and be right back. We'll bury the body later."

Laughter bubbled up through Callie as she stepped forward. "Go answer it. It's not like I won't still be here when they leave. I sleep here, remember?"

His eyes darkened as he narrowed his gaze on her erect nipples, which were apparent through the cotton shirt.

The doorbell chimed again and he growled, "I'm so not in the mood for visitors."

Callie looked down at the bulge in his shorts. "Why don't you let me get it while you start reciting the Gettysburg Address again? That should help you…settle down."

As she walked from the room, Noah's bark of laughter trailed down the wide hallway. No matter that her day wasn't what she wanted it to be; Noah always managed to make her smile. She only hoped she could do the same for him. If she did it enough, maybe she could help him get past whatever it was that plagued him.

Callie glanced out the sidelight and saw Max. There wasn't a woman in Hollywood, or most of the world for that matter, that didn't love Max Ford. The man was not only one of the best actors in the business; he was drop-dead, curl-your-toes, giggly-schoolgirl gorgeous. But while Callie didn't deny the fact he was a very sexy piece of scenery, he didn't give her those flutters like Noah did.

Oh, God. She knew she'd been infatuated with Noah and enjoyed the sex, but…flutters? Was she feeling something more for her boss, caregiver, lover?

Shoving aside the epiphany and fear, she pulled open the door.

Max's eyes were shielded by a dark pair of sunglasses and he wasn't smiling. The man was always grinning, even when he talked; that was all part of his charm

"What's wrong?"

"Is Noah here?"

Callie stepped aside. "He's in the gym. Everything okay?"

Without an answer, Max took off down the hall, and Callie didn't know whether she should follow. This really wasn't her business, but at the same time she knew Noah had had a rough day and she didn't want him to have to receive more bad news. Whatever it might be.

But as she walked down the hall toward the gym, she heard the word *cancer* and froze. Did Max have cancer? She tried not to eavesdrop…okay, she didn't try, but she felt guilty for it and that was close enough. As she went to the door, she heard Max say *mother* and that was all she needed to hear to realize this was not her place.

Poor Max. He'd looked helpless when she'd opened the door and she'd never seen him look anything but charming, sexy and smiling.…

She made her way to the office where Noah had told her she could use his desktop computer instead of the laptop in the kitchen nook. The office was dark with navy walls, exposed walnut beams overhead and on the floor, but it was the floor-to-ceiling windows behind his desk that really opened up the room.

If she was serious about not working for him, she really needed to start looking to branch out somehow. Perhaps with her teaching degree she didn't have to limit herself to public schools. She could teach at handicapped schools or even work in an office at a school. The possibilities were there; she just had to explore them.

More than that, though, she needed to look at her life differently now. As much as she wanted to get her face back to normal, to get her life back to where it had been, she had to face the reality that this might not happen. Ever.

Noah had mentioned considering surgery soon and the thought terrified her. Oh, she wasn't afraid of pain, not to her face, anyway. She was terrified of the pain in her heart she'd endure if the surgery failed. She just couldn't get her hopes up.

She logged on to the internet and looked at job postings for the schools in the surrounding area, shocked to see how many there were. She could even go a bit farther out of L.A. There wasn't anything holding her here anymore.

First she'd have to write up a really nice résumé, and then she'd have to see if Noah would write her a letter of recommendation.

She eased back in the leather office chair and sighed. There was a major part of her that wanted to toss that computer across the room, but this life she now faced was her fault. She'd been so wrapped up in wanting to be the next big star that she'd never planned for anything else.

Oh, her parents made her get an education, but she'd never even created a résumé using that degree because she never thought she'd need it. Callie had never had any intention of becoming a schoolteacher.

Good thing she'd listened to her parents.

She reached up, lightly touching the imperfection down the side of her face. She tried to avoid mirrors, and since she was temporarily living with a man, that wasn't too hard, because they weren't all over the house. But there was one on the far wall by the entry to the office. The mirror was actually rather large and Callie figured Noah's interior designer probably put that there so the light coming in the windows across the room would bounce off the mirror.

Callie eased from the seat and made her way over. She

wasn't scared, not like she'd been those first few days of looking at herself after she'd get out of the shower. There was no surprise that was going to be waiting for her once she saw her reflection.

She approached the mirror and sighed as she closed that final distance. The ugly red, puckered line running from her temple down to her jawline, thankfully missing her eye, stared back at her. Callie turned slightly to take a better look. She supposed it was looking better, but not nearly what she wanted. Even if she parted her hair on a different side and covered the scar for casting calls, she'd have to let it show at some point. Not all roles would have her hair down, clinging to the right side of her face.

She reached up gently, using her right hand, and traced the jagged line. Her shoulder was healing beautifully and was almost as good as new. Her face…well, that was still something Noah didn't discuss too much and she didn't know if he just didn't want to upset her or if he was afraid to tell her the truth.

She chose to believe the latter even though she'd never taken him for a coward.

Noah stepped into the room and came to stand behind her. "Staring at it will not make it go away," he told her.

"I know." Callie nodded, holding his gaze in the mirror. "How's Max?"

"Scared, worried. His mother has cancer."

"I heard him tell you that, so I decided to leave you two alone."

Noah rested his hands on her shoulders and eased her against his chest. "That means a lot to me that you knew we needed that time alone."

Callie drew her brows together. "Of course you needed to be alone. He's your best friend and he's dealing with life-altering news."

He stared at her in the mirror and sighed. "I've just never

known anyone like you, Callie. In the office you were an awe-some employee and someone I wanted to know better, but now that I've gotten to know you even more, I can honestly say you're amazing."

Compliments made her uncomfortable, so she didn't reply.

"I'm glad you're here," he whispered as he slid her hair aside and kissed the side of her neck. "And I'm positive we were working on something very encouraging before that doorbell rang."

Shivers slid through Callie's body as she relaxed fully against him. "You've had such a stressful day, Noah. Why don't you let me—"

"I know exactly what you can be doing and it involves si-lence," he whispered against her ear before he placed a warm kiss in that very delicate, erotic area.

"What are we doing?" she asked.

"I'm about to get you naked."

She sighed and smiled. "I mean, what are we doing? Is this a relationship or are we just having a good time?"

He froze, bringing his eyes up to the mirror. "I can't an-swer that right now, but I can tell you I'm happy when you're with me and I'm happy you're here. Not with the circum-stances, but I like having you in my house."

She didn't say anything, wasn't quite sure how to respond to his lack of commitment.

"I'm sorry," he told her. "I just can't give you more right now."

Callie smiled. "It's okay. You're honest. I'd rather that than you telling me what you think I want to hear."

"Are you done talking?" he asked, the corners of his mouth tilting up.

Callie grinned. "I'm done. Now, what were you about to show me in that workout room before Max came?"

"I was about to show you how good we are together."

Callie tried not to let those promising words into her heart, but she couldn't keep them back. He'd turned them loose and like an arrow, they shot straight to the target.

But she knew he didn't mean that like it sounded. She also knew they *were* good together and she wanted to explore the possibility that this might not be as temporary as either of them had thought.

Noah's talented lips cruised from her mouth down her throat and into the V of the oversize shirt. She loved wearing his shirts, always having that little piece of him right next to her bare skin at all times.

She gripped his shoulders as he undid each button and slid the garment off and to the floor.

In seconds, he'd turned her to face him and crushed his mouth onto hers. Chest to chest, she arched against his warm body, thankful he'd been about to work out and he'd forgone the shirt.

Without breaking the kiss, he shoved her shorts and panties down. She helped by wiggling until they were at her feet and she flicked them aside with her toes. She helped rid him of his shorts as well after he'd kicked off his tennis shoes.

"I love the way you taste," he murmured against her lips. "I can't get enough."

Neither could she.

He bent and scooped her up in that romantic gesture she'd only seen on TV or read in books. And when he sat her on the edge of his desk, she grinned up at him.

"We never make it to a bed."

He smiled. "I have six bedrooms and they're all too far away."

Callie looped her good arm around his shoulders and gripped his neck as she slid her body forward, closer to his. She wanted him so badly. She'd never felt this way before.

Never known she could lose control so quickly or fall so hard for one man.

But there was no lying to herself anymore. The way he looked at her, cared for her and cherished her made her realize she was totally in love with Noah Foster.

The thought terrified her. Could she seriously risk her heart, her emotional state, on another dream that might not come true?

But for right now, she wanted him and she would take what she could get.

"Condom?" she asked.

He rested his forehead against hers. "In my bedroom."

She bit her lip and said, "I'm clean, Noah. I've only been with two people other than you and I've always used protection. Plus, I have an IUD."

His lips pressed to hers. "I've always used protection, too, but this is your call."

Without using words, she gave him her answer when she locked her ankles around his back. As he drove into her, he slid one hand behind her back and another hand beneath her hair, bringing her mouth to his.

Their bodies moved so beautifully together, Callie knew this man was the one for her. Perfection didn't happen with anything in life, but this coming together was as near to perfect as she could get.

With her ankles secure behind him, she arched farther, pulling him deeper and moaning into his mouth as her climax edged closer.

Noah's body quickened as he tore his mouth free. He rested his forehead against hers and their gazes locked for a second. In his eyes she saw not the pain that usually hid there, but something deeper. Something she doubted he knew he felt.

For that one brief second, she saw love.

Callie's body quivered as she let her orgasm roll through

her. Noah's body tightened with hers and he squeezed his eyes shut.

He might not want to admit or even acknowledge what had just happened or what he'd been feeling, but Callie knew in her heart that Noah was falling for her. Now she just had to make sure whatever hell his past kept him in didn't break either of them.

Thirteen

Callie felt like a little girl again. As she pulled her rental car into the drive of her Kansas home, all her childhood memories flooded her.

Sure enough, a giant blue tarp covered the roof at the end of the house, right over where her bedroom used to be. Of course that was where the roof would choose to blow off. Fate wasn't being kind lately and this was just par for the course.

Mentally, Callie gave fate the one-fingered salute and laughed—it was either that or cry at the image of rainwater filling her bedroom, making even her past life a mess.

As she exited the car, her mother and father came out onto the porch and all that worry with the roof, with the accident and the lost movie part were pushed to the back of her mind. She'd missed them. Even though she hadn't grown up with the best of everything, her parents had always been there. Even when she'd felt fat and like an outcast, her parents had urged her to better herself, always seeing the brighter side of her.

Callie dropped her bag on the ground beside the steps and reached for her mother with her left arm. When her father moved in for a hug on her right side, Callie stepped back.

"Sorry, I'm still a little sore from the broken collarbone." She tried to smile, but both her parents zeroed in on her cheek. "It's not as bad as it looks. Just healing kind of ugly."

Her mother teared up. "Oh, baby. I'm so sorry you were hurt."

Callie waved it off because she did not come home for pity; she came to help and that was precisely what she'd concentrate on.

"I'm fine. Really. Noah has plans to fix this once it's ready for surgery." Not that he could make her perfect again, but she doubted her parents knew that. "So, what's the cost of the roof going to be?"

Her father sighed. "A buddy I used to work with said he could help replace it, but the materials are still costly. We're hoping to just get that side done for now, but another bad storm and the rest could go."

Bad storm? In Kansas? Yeah, the chances of that were well over 100 percent.

Callie nodded. "Then we'll find a way to get this done," she told them. "I have a little money left. Not much after my plane ticket, but I'll make some calls and see what I can do."

Her father wrapped his arm around her. "Honey, we didn't expect you to rush home. There's nothing you can do that I couldn't do."

"True, but I feel better knowing I'm here helping you guys."

Her father stared down at her and then smiled. "You always were such a fighter and so determined. I'm glad you're home, Callie."

Yeah, that was her. Determined and a fighter. Too bad she'd

been sitting around wallowing in self-pity over this accident. But now she'd at least feel as if she was helping.

And she wasn't even going to ask if her sister had helped. More than likely she didn't even know how bad off Mom and Dad were.

"Let's get inside and catch up," her mother said, reaching for the bag. "I want to hear all about Hollywood and the glamorous things you've seen."

Okay, that was a topic she could definitely discuss because the things she'd seen in that office were fodder for girlie gossip and she could use the laughs with her mother.

The trip alone would be good for her. She needed time away from L.A., from Noah. And spending the evening with her mother was the perfect way to help her clear her mind.

Callie had forgotten how much she missed home-cooked food. Her mother had made biscuits from scratch and gravy with eggs and sausage. There was nothing like a meal full of carbs and calories to have her slipping into a state of euphoria while snuggled on the old, comfy couch watching television—an old war movie, of course.

Her mother sat beside her, and her father had planted himself in his recliner. Yeah, this was the simple life she both did and did not miss. It was nice to come home and get back to the simplicity, but at the same time, Callie knew she did not want to grow up and live in a small town where the most exciting thing in the evening was watching the news or doing crossword puzzles.

The doorbell cut through the room, causing the three of them to turn their attention toward the front door.

"Wonder who that is," her father mumbled as he went to the door.

Callie remained in her seat as her father flicked the dead bolt and opened the door.

"Excuse me, sir."

Oh, God. She knew that voice.

"I'm looking for Callie Matthews."

She jumped to her feet, pulled her T-shirt down and stepped up beside her father. "Noah! What are you doing here?"

Dear Lord, she wanted the earth to open up and swallow her, but at the same time she was so shocked at his presence she didn't know how to act. Inside she was jumping up and down with joy that he'd taken the initiative to come all the way here, but she didn't want him to feel obligated to help her.

"Noah?" her father asked, opening the door wider. "This is the doctor you work for?"

Callie nodded, keeping her eyes fixed on Noah, who looked so…down-to-earth in his worn jeans, tennis shoes, plain gray T-shirt and a bag slung over his shoulder. If she didn't know he was a top Hollywood surgeon, she'd guess he lived right here in Kansas.

"Come in, come in," her mother chimed from behind her. "Don't leave the poor man on the porch."

Callie glanced around to the tidy, yet very well-worn living room. Nothing matched and all the furniture was from her childhood. But she refused to be embarrassed about her humble beginnings. This was the life she knew before meeting him, and while she might not want to be at this point anymore in her life, she wasn't ashamed, either.

"I thought I could help." Noah set his bag on the floor by the door. "Since you wouldn't let me come with you, I thought I'd surprise you."

Callie laughed. "I'm surprised, all right. I assume you looked up my emergency contact on my file at work to get the address?"

Noah smiled and that high-voltage smile was all Hollywood and should've been in front of cameras instead of hiding behind a surgical mask.

"I tend to get what I want," he told her, holding her gaze for a brief moment. Then he turned his attention to her father and held out his hand. "We haven't been properly introduced. I'm Noah Foster."

"Jim Matthews," her father said, pumping Noah's hand. "And this is my wife, Erma."

"Pleasure to meet you," Noah told her parents. "I don't want to intrude, so after I talk with Callie for a bit, I'll just find the closest hotel. But I meant it when I said I could help."

"You'll not stay at a hotel," her mother scolded. "We may be down a bedroom because of the roof, but we still have the bedroom in the basement. You're more than welcome to stay here. Are you hungry? We just had dinner and there's some left over."

Noah shook his head, smile still in place. "No, ma'am. I grabbed something when my plane landed."

As Noah charmed her parents, Callie stood frozen. Noah Foster was in her living room talking to her parents as if he belonged here.

Her father's voice broke into her thoughts. "Callie, honey, why don't you show Noah the bedroom he can use downstairs?"

"Of course." She moved around the group and headed down the narrow hallway. "Come on, Noah. We can talk down here."

She opened the basement door and flicked on the light to descend the steps. Once she hit the bottom, she turned on another light that illuminated the bedroom.

"It's pretty bare," she told him when he joined her. "We don't usually have company. My bedroom is out of commission, so I'll be taking the couch."

He jerked his head toward her. "Couch? I'll just go to a hotel, or I can take the couch."

Callie shook her head. "Don't be silly. You're here and this room is all yours…unless you want something fancier."

Noah dropped his bag on the worn carpet and stepped closer. "Callie, I think you know me well enough by now to realize that I'm not a snob. I didn't fly all this way to be pampered or treated like a socialite. I came to help you in any way I can. I know you are here to help your parents. I care for you and I'm here for you. Don't shut me out because you're ashamed of where you came from."

Callie looked away, unable to hold his gaze.. He tapped beneath her chin with his finger until she looked up at him.

"Now, instead of the couch or the hotel, why don't we just share this room?"

"Because I'm not shacking up with you while my parents are in the same house."

Noah laughed. "You think they are unaware that you're not a virgin?"

"I'm sure they know I'm not, but still."

He quirked a brow. "Still what? I want you in bed with me, Callie. We can…talk. That way tomorrow we will be ready to tackle whatever needs to be done."

On a groan, Callie reached up with one hand and toyed with his dark hair. "I can't believe you flew all this way to help me when you don't even know what you're helping with."

He shrugged. "I assume it has something to do with that big blue tarp on the house?"

"Yeah." She sighed. "The storm the other night took off a portion of the roof that was over my bedroom."

"So they need a new roof? What's the cost?"

"Dad has a friend who will help him replace the roof, but the materials are still so costly." Callie dropped her hand and picked up Noah's bag, placing it on the small dresser. "I plan to go to the bank tomorrow to see about a small loan to help them. I'm not sure if I can get one, but I know that my credit is better than theirs, and with my dad still unemployed—"

"You need to relax," he told her. "This will all work out. Why don't you go take a bath and read a book? I know you love to read."

Callie smiled. "I would love to go be lazy for a few minutes, but I'm not leaving you alone with my parents."

He moved toward her, wrapping his arms around her waist. "Why? Afraid they'll pull out the baby pictures or embarrassing school photos?"

"To be honest, yes." She slid her hands up his arms. "You wouldn't recognize the girl I used to be."

Noah's lips softly touched hers before he pulled her into a warm embrace. "I'm sure the same loving, caring, bright spirit would be looking back at me in those pictures."

Callie inhaled the sexy, masculine aroma that she'd become familiar with since being with Noah. "You may be surprised."

"I promise not to look at any pictures," he told her, easing back. "Now, go relax in the tub and grab a book. Your parents and I will be just fine."

Callie hesitated, but she was tired, and if she was going to actually sleep down here with Noah, she'd at least like to freshen up first.

Lord help her. Noah must really care for her to show up like this, but she feared reading too much into this surprise. No matter her feelings, she couldn't assume he felt the same.

Noah had set his plan in motion and now all he had to do was wait for Callie to come back downstairs. After a brief yet detailed talk with her father, Noah was ready to enjoy his time with Callie. Alone. Naked.

While he'd been upstairs he'd seen a few random snapshots of the family over the years. He had to assume the overweight girl in the photos was Callie because the tall blonde certainly wasn't and the only other kid in the pictures was a boy. No wonder she said he wouldn't recognize her. She was quite heavy, but she'd still been beautiful and that smile had been just as radiant.

He heard Callie upstairs in the kitchen speaking with her mother, but couldn't make out the words. After about an hour, she came down wearing an old, baggy T-shirt and a pair of boxer shorts. She was the sexiest sight he'd ever seen.

"I wasn't expecting a sleepover," she explained. "I knew I had old clothes here, so I didn't pack pajamas."

Noah remained seated on the edge of the bed. "Don't apologize for being you, Callie."

"These were some of my fat clothes," she told him, holding on to the newel post. "Since you're here, you might as well know more about me and why I fought so hard to get out of this town."

Noah waited because he could see her searching within herself to find the courage to speak up. He was surprised at how deeply he wanted to get to know her.

"I was quite overweight growing up," she began. "I wasn't popular, I didn't feel like I belonged, especially being a middle child, and I knew I would leave this town as soon as possible.

"I used to watch old movies while all the other teenagers were at parties or ball games. I would fantasize about being a star, wonder how awesome it would be to make a name for myself."

Callie sat on the bottom step. "My parents were adamant I get a college education. Through financial aid I got my bachelor's in Early Childhood Development, but I knew I didn't want to be a teacher. I wanted to be an actress. I also knew that with my appearance, Hollywood wouldn't look twice in my direction."

The picture she was painting made Noah's heart ache for

her. He was getting a glimpse inside this little girl's dream and the woman who had to face reality.

"The entire time I was in college I worked out and ate right," she went on. "By the end of my four years, I was a totally different person. And after I graduated, I continued to work for the college in the office until I could save enough money to move to L.A."

Her eyes drifted across the room to his. The entire time she'd been talking she'd focused her attention away from him, as if she was afraid to see his reaction.

"Why are you acting worried and ashamed of what I may think?" he finally asked. "Does it truly matter what I think, Callie? Or anyone else for that matter? All this story does is prove to me that you're a fighter."

She shrugged. "That may be, but fighting won't change anything now."

Noah came to his feet, crossed the room and took hold of her hands until she stood in front of him. "You may be right, but if you want a job in the movie industry, then you'll get one. You just have that personality. It's like mine. No matter the odds, we don't back down from what we want."

Callie studied his face. "What odds were ever stacked against you?"

He wasn't ready to open up about Malinda so he decided to share a different problem. "I can't live up to this hero-worship status that Blake has me at," he explained, baring a piece of his own fears. "No matter how I go about performing surgery on this little guy, he's still going to have scars, and the harsh truth is, kids will be kids and he will probably be stared at when he goes back to school. I can only minimize the damage."

But Noah would give anything to be able to make the child perfect again. And Callie.

Callie stroked his cheek. "You're doing all you can and he

sees that. His mother sees that. Any improvement will make him happy. You need to believe that."

Noah grabbed her hand, kissed her palm and tugged her against his chest. "What I believe is that I need you. Here. Now."

She wrapped her arms around his waist and her floral aroma from her soap or shampoo enveloped him. He'd warned himself not to get too involved with this woman, yet when he knew she was worried for her family and needed to take off halfway across the country, he hadn't thought twice about joining her.

The fact that he was in deeper than he'd ever imagined scared him, but he wouldn't let fear override the need, the passion and the special bond he shared with Callie.

Callie's mouth hovered over his. "Make love to me, Noah."

He didn't need any more of an invitation.

Callie woke to the sound of pounding and banging and glanced to the bedside clock.

Nearly ten? She rubbed her eyes and looked again. She'd never, ever slept this late. The opposite side of the bed was empty, and when she ran her hand over the sheet, she found it to be cold, which told her Noah had been up for some time.

After she changed into jeans and a more fitted T-shirt, she flipped her head upside down so she could pull her hair up without reaching so far.

No one was in the house so she assumed they were all outside with the commotion. But the sight she saw when she stepped off the porch was one she'd never forget for as long as she lived.

Not only was her father up on the roof with his friend who'd offered to help, her brother was there and…Noah? For real? The man had a steady hand with a scalpel and a syringe full of Botox. He didn't go around wielding hammers.

But he did look mighty fine with his sweat-stained gray T-shirt and muscles flexing as he pulled off the old shingles and tossed them into the yard.

He caught sight of her and smiled. It was the same smile he'd given her as they'd made love, the same smile she noticed he seemed to keep in reserve for just her...because there was heat and, dare she hope, promise behind that grin.

"Morning, sis," her brother greeted. "What happened to your face?"

Callie sighed. Apparently, her parents hadn't said anything to him. "Car accident."

Her brother nodded and went back to ripping off shingles and tossing them. Apparently, a twenty-two-year-old didn't think twice about her accident or the impact it had on her life.

"Did we wake you?" Noah called down from the roof.

Callie shielded her eyes from the bright morning sun. "I should've been up before now. Can I talk to you just a moment when you can take a break?"

Noah laid his hammer on the roof and climbed down the ladder.

"Don't keep him too long," her father shouted down. "We don't have all day. Your doc has to leave for the big city tomorrow."

Callie smiled at her father, grabbed Noah's hand and took him around to the side of the house.

"What in the world is going on?" she asked.

"If you'll let me get back up there, a new roof is going on."

Callie propped her hands on her hips and rolled her eyes. "Obviously, but where did the miracle funds and materials come from, and more important, why didn't I know you could play carpenter, too?"

Noah slid an arm around her waist. "Ready to see me in my tool belt?"

Trying to hold back a smile, and failing, she placed a hand

on his chest. "Simmer down, lover boy. I didn't know you knew how to replace a roof."

He shrugged. "I don't, but I can follow directions and they need the help."

Callie's heart clenched. As if she hadn't already been head over heels, the man's simple declaration reached in, grabbed her heart and took it all for himself.

"Where did that truck full of new shingles come from?" she asked, trying not to put her heart on her sleeve.

"I called the local home-renovation store last night, put everything on my credit card and asked for immediate delivery."

Flabbergasted, she gripped the arm that he still had locked around her waist. "How did you know what to order and when did you do all of this?"

"I talked with your father while you were in the shower and he told me what was needed."

Callie quirked a brow. "My father just let you, a stranger to him, come in and pay for all of this?"

Noah's eyes softened. "I may have mentioned we were closer than employee/employer and I had no real family of my own and I wanted to help."

Tears lodged in her throat as wave after wave of emotions slammed into her. Gratitude and love played the biggest role.

"I can't even..." Callie turned her head, swallowed back tears and met his gaze again. "I can't begin to tell you what this means to me, to my family."

Noah swiped her damp cheek and kissed her gently. "I didn't want this to happen. This relationship we have. I fought against it, but you do something to me, Callie, and when you need anything, I want to be the one who provides it for you."

Oh, God. Did he mean...

"I'm glad I could help," he went on. "But I do have to get back to L.A tomorrow. I plan to meet with Blake very early Monday morning so we can go over his pre-op plan."

Callie nodded, cupped Noah's face and slid her lips over his. "Get back to work."

As he walked away, Callie couldn't help but wonder where his feelings had landed him. Did he love her and was just afraid to say it?

She knew one thing for sure, though. When they got back to L.A. they had a major talk in their future.

When she'd first had her accident she thought for sure all was lost, but in some weird, twisted way, had this damage to her life opened her eyes wider to what was really important? Had this tragedy brought her and Noah together more strongly than would have been possible before?

For the first time in weeks, Callie had a new hope for her future, and that fighter in her was back full force.

"Callie."

She glanced up to see her mother coming around the side of the house.

"Hey, Mama."

Erma smiled. "Why don't you come inside with me and we can start preparing a nice, big lunch because our men will be ready to eat in a couple hours?"

Callie shook her head. "Oh, Noah's not my man, Mom."

Reaching out, her mother smoothed her hair off her forehead and nodded. "Oh, he is. You wouldn't have slept downstairs with him and he wouldn't be here helping if he weren't yours. Besides, I saw the way he looked at you. That man has much more than lust in his eyes, Callie Ray. He has love."

Callie stared at her mother, unable to speak. Love? Dare she hope?

"Now, come on in," Erma said, looping her arm through Callie's. "And tell me all about your hunky doctor."

Fourteen

Noah had taken off as much time as possible and Callie's arm was healing nicely, though he still managed to find reasons to assist her and he was pleasantly surprised she let him.

But he'd gone back to work today with his regular hours and the load was full, which meant he left the office later than he wanted to. Marie was wonderful, but he missed seeing Callie's bright, chipper smile at the front desk.

Truth was, he missed Callie. Period. Their relationship had changed the last time they'd been intimate. A change he wasn't ready for and certainly couldn't define. But there was another level of trust, of caring. And that was a place he couldn't visit, couldn't think about and couldn't get wrapped up in. This had to be just sex.

Tonight, though, he had a surprise for his houseguest.

When he finally pulled into his garage, he nearly sighed with relief. He loved his job, truly he did, but after two and a half weeks of staying home with Callie, he found he'd spoiled himself.

He was anxious to see Callie's reaction to her gift. Though the pool table might have been his best gift ever, he was still eager to see how she would react to something more...personal.

When he stepped into the house from the garage, he didn't spot her right away.

"Callie?" he called as he walked through the foyer and headed up the stairs.

He didn't find her in the living room or her bedroom. Curious, he went outside, and sure enough she was lounging by the pool wearing a loose halter top and matching shorts. The sun had kissed her skin, and her nose was a subtle shade of pink. He assumed she'd put her antibiotic ointment on her scar, so she should be fine, but if she turned red, he'd have to get her inside.

"Getting some sun?" he asked, coming to sit on the foot of the chaise longue.

She'd been reading and she put the book across her stomach. "Trying to. I was starting to look pretty pale."

His eyes traveled down her legs and back up. "Looking pretty good to me."

With a soft smile, she eased forward. "How was your first full day back to work?"

"Everyone asked about you," he told her. "They all wanted to know when you were coming back. I told them I wasn't sure."

Callie sighed. "Why didn't you just tell them the truth? I'm not coming back."

"You might. The only person stopping you is you."

She motioned to her face. "No, this is stopping me."

"A scar?" he asked. "You would be so surprised at how many people will be glad to see you and that you're healing.

Please, at least try to come back for one day a week and we'll go from there."

Callie glanced out to the waterfall trickling into the pool. "I'm not sure, Noah. I don't even want to go out to the grocery store, much less work in an office full of beautiful people."

Noah took her hand, pulled her to her feet as he stood. Her book fell to the stone patio.

"Wait," she told him before he could pull her away. "I'm not saying that to anger you, really I'm not. I just don't want you to think me working in your office is a long-term thing or something I'll be comfortable doing. Even if I did come back for one day a week, I still wouldn't be staying there."

He admired her—how could he not? But he was so damn tired of her thinking her beauty was superficial.

"I want to take you somewhere."

She started to protest, but he held up his other hand. "I promise no one will see you, but even if they did, they'd think you were beautiful just like I do. You don't even need to change."

She slid into her flip-flops and followed him through the house and to the garage.

"But aren't you tired?" she asked as they got into the car.

"Not too tired for this."

Somehow they'd arrived at a deeper emotional relationship than just colleagues or friends. He didn't know where it would lead, but it was past time she learned a bit more about him, about why he was so adamant that she realize beauty was from within and there was so much more to life.

He hit the freeway and blended into the thick traffic, all the while hoping he didn't infringe on some unspoken code of plastic-surgeon ethics.

Callie wasn't going to believe his platitudes just because he kept preaching them. She needed a visual and he planned to give her just that.

"Where are we going?"

He threw her a sideways glance and a smile. "I knew you couldn't just sit back and enjoy the ride."

"Well, you're right. So, where are we going?" she repeated.

"We're going to a place that will remind us both of how something good can come out of a bad situation."

Callie sighed and leaned against the door. "I'd rather be home."

The word caused a tightening in his stomach that caught him off guard. By *home,* she meant his house, not her apartment.

He didn't comment, didn't really know what to say, but he was glad she was comfortable and felt as if she could call that her home.

But she'd still never been in the bedroom that he'd shared with Malinda.

He pulled into a familiar subdivision and found the place he was looking for.

"Here we are," he told her as he shut off the car. "Come on in."

Callie looked at the stone-and-brick home that was obviously fairly new and beyond gorgeous. Then she jerked her gaze back to his.

"Wait," she said, reaching for his arm. "Come in? Who lives here? You said I didn't have to see anybody."

"I own this house," he told her before he got out. "This is the one that has sat empty."

Callie opened her car door and followed Noah up the thin steps to the front door with a small stained-glass window adorning the top.

He unlocked the door and gestured her in first.

"Noah, this house is stunning." She moved through the open floor plan, trying to take in the giant room all at once. "I love how this is all so cozy, yet open."

There was a tall stone wall only a few feet wide that was the center of the main floor and somewhat separated the living area and the dining room and kitchen. Water trickled down the stone, making her instantly relax. The neutral colors weren't masculine or harsh.

She turned back to him. "This house is so different from your other one."

He nodded. "That's because I had this one built to my specifications after my first house on this property nearly washed away."

"Washed away?"

He motioned for her to enter the living area on the other side of the stone waterfall.

"This was the first house I purchased after I started my practice." He pointed to a picture on the end table. "I lived here about five years before flooding took it. I remember thinking that I had nothing but an empty, muddy lot."

Callie stared at the photo, trying to even fathom a house simply washing away.

"I didn't realize there was a flooding problem out here."

He came to stand beside her. "The drainage isn't great, so if it rains too much, too fast, we have floods."

She turned to face him. "I know you're trying to teach me a lesson here, but I'm not getting it."

His bright eyes bored into hers as he rested his hands on her shoulders. "I had an ugly thing happen in my life and I had a choice of whether I wanted to let it consume me and feel sorry for myself or if I wanted to take control of my life and turn this unwelcome disaster into something positive."

Callie glanced to the picture and back to him. "Are you comparing me to this house?"

He turned her body to face the stone centerpiece again and eased her closer.

"That stone was all I had left when my home was destroyed," he told her. "I used all I had to rebuild my life. But I not only rebuilt it, I made it better."

His words hit her straight in her heart. She wanted to rebuild her life, truly she didn't want to be that person who sat around and cried for herself, but she had no clue how to rebuild.

"If I thought I could take my life and make it better, Noah, I would."

He eased her back around to face him as he gathered her into his warm, caring embrace.

"It will be better." He kissed the top of her head and eased back. "The microdermabrasion went well and we can do another soon. I've talked with a few colleagues and we all seem to think that will make a tremendous difference over the next few months until we can further explore surgery options…if we even have to go that route."

Callie tensed. "Really? You think surgery may not be needed?"

"The swelling is gone in the tissues beneath the laceration and the wound isn't as deep as we'd first thought. The healing is looking remarkable."

Tears burned Callie's eyes. "I want to hope, Noah. I don't even mind surgery. I just want to be me again, but I'm afraid."

Noah tilted her face up to his and captured her lips. Softly, lovingly he coaxed her lips apart and showed her how he felt.

"I'm not afraid, Callie," he whispered. "I'm excited for your future. This is going to work and we are going to battle it together."

She lifted her lids and looked him in the eye. "You're always such a confident doctor."

"I won't lie to you," he told her, still framing her face with his hands. "It will take time. But I believe we can really make this minimal. The wound itself isn't as bad as I'd first thought."

Callie nodded and smiled as a tear slid down her cheek. Noah swiped it away with the pad of his thumb.

"I trust you."

She slid her arms around his neck and toyed with the ends of his hair. His hands spanned her waist as he pulled her fully against him.

"I want you," he murmured. "In my house, with the sunset coming in that window. I want you, Callie."

Shivers slid over and through her body at his honest, raw words. "Then have me."

Noah captured her mouth again and walked her back to the living area, where he eased her down onto the cushy chaise. Noah pulled his polo off, flinging it to the side.

Callie stared up at him in all his golden, muscular glory. As he finished undressing, her heart picked up just a bit faster and her body quivered with anticipation. Each time they were intimate, each time they took their relationship to another level, she wanted to know where this was headed. But right now she only wanted one thing. Noah.

With ease, she took off her halter top, exposing her bare breasts to his appraisal, and tossed the unwanted garment to the floor with his clothes. Noah held his hand out and she took it as he helped her to her feet. After sliding out of her shorts and flicking them off to the side with her toe, she moved to mold her body against his. She never got used to how amazing that initial contact felt. Never got over that first feeling of how right it was being with Noah.

Callie threaded her hands through his hair and pulled his mouth down to hers. Noah's strong hands covered her back, his fingertips gripping her. Her breasts flattened against his chest, her hips bumped his. And it was still not enough. Not close enough, not emotional enough. She wanted more.

"Noah," she whispered against his lips. "I need you to know—"

"Shh." He nipped at her lips again. "Later."

Callie wasn't sure if she should tell him she was in love with him or if fate had just saved her from making a fool of herself. But when his hands came down to grip her rear and lift her off the floor, she didn't care.

Noah eased a knee onto the chaise and he slowly laid her down, never breaking their contact. He didn't want to break this bond, didn't want to ruin this perfection. If he could crawl inside this moment in time and live here forever, he would. Right now, at this second, he was happier than he'd been in a long, long time. He owed Callie so much for showing him how to live again. This little trip to the old house wasn't just an eye-opening experience for her; reality had also slapped him in the face. He'd come to the conclusion that no matter what he'd lost, he could still make that decision to move forward or let the past consume him.

And right now he was making the decision to make love to Callie in his living room.

"I want you. Here. Now."

And that was all Noah needed to hear before he slid into her, without the barrier, without anything between them, just like the past two times.

But this time was different. He'd laid his heart out there for her to see and that vulnerability could get him hurt again. But he couldn't stop this emotional spiral he was on when it came to Callie and her sweet, sometimes innocent ways.

His body moved over hers, but he was careful to hold himself up on his elbows. He didn't want to crush her, but seeing her look up at him, with all the trust and love in her eyes…

Love?

Yes. When he looked at her, he saw love. And if he were honest with himself, he'd seen it in Kansas, too.

Noah kissed her, unable to look into those expressive eyes

for another moment, because what if she could read his? What would she see?

His tongue mimicked their bodies as he increased the pace and her ankles locked together behind his back.

Before he could think too much about what he'd seen, her body tightened around him, causing him to lose control and give in to the pleasure that only Callie could provide.

As his body settled half on hers, half off, he tried to shut out the fact that every time he closed his eyes and thought of a woman in his life, Malinda wasn't even in the mental picture. Callie filled his mind. She was filling his bed, his house, and he feared she'd fill his heart if he let her.

Fifteen

Callie ran her fingertips up Noah's back, but she had a feeling he'd fallen asleep. His breathing had slowed and his body had relaxed against hers some time ago. And even though her belly growled, she didn't care. The sun had set and they were lying in the dark, completely naked, and she finally saw a sliver of hope in this darkness she'd been living in. Could they have a future together? He seemed to not even worry about her looks, the scarring.

Admitting to herself that she was in love with Noah didn't frighten her or make her wonder about their future. He might not admit he had feelings for her, but she knew in her heart that he felt something beyond friendship or he wouldn't be so giving, so patient and caring with her. He'd totally put all her needs first for the past several weeks, even choosing to take care of her over going into the office.

The man who was known for dating a different woman nearly every night and during the day making his clients perfectly beautiful was now devoting all of his time to her. Callie knew he had deep feelings for her, but she also figured that past, and that photo in his room, kept him from moving forward. She only hoped he'd open up to her, let her further into this world of his she so desperately wanted to be part of.

But she wouldn't be that clingy woman, wouldn't be the one who put her heart out there with the possibility it could get stomped into unrecognizable pieces.

"Thelma," Noah murmured in his sleep. "Don't. Please."

Callie sat up, shifting Noah's body a little more off her and onto the oversize chaise. She looked down to his tortured face, his brows drawn together, his jaw clenched.

"No," he cried. "Don't worry."

Callie shook his shoulder. "Noah. Noah, wake up."

He muttered something else she couldn't quite make out and the intense look on his face tore at Callie's heart.

Shaking him harder with one hand, Callie tapped at his cheek with her other. "Noah. You're dreaming."

His lids fluttered open, his eyes darted to hers, held there, and then he closed his eyes again.

"Damn," he whispered.

Callie wasn't sure how to proceed on this shaky ground, but she wasn't backing down.

"Care to tell me what just happened?"

Noah shook his head, running a hand down his face. "Just dreaming about Thelma."

Callie nodded. "I got that. Who is she to you?"

His gaze met hers. "She's the lady at the assisted-living facility I visit."

Noah got up, walked naked through the room and rummaged around to find his pants, using only the pale glow of the distant city lights cutting through the windows.

Callie eased back on the chaise, hoping he'd elaborate

more, needing to understand why this woman who wasn't even a blood relative was in his nightmares.

"So, how does she have such a hold on you?"

Noah pulled up his dress pants, leaving them unbuttoned, and rested his hands on his hips. Callie watched as he struggled with himself. He lowered his head between his shoulders and rubbed the back of his neck.

"It's a long story, Callie, and one I'm just not comfortable getting into."

Hurt filled her, tugging at her heart she'd so freely given to him.

"I'd like to think we are here for each other, Noah. I want to help, but you won't let me in."

He turned to face her, that look of torment still all over his face. "If I could let anybody in, Callie, it would be you."

Callie came to her feet. That declaration was bittersweet. She knew he wanted to open up, but something in his past simply wouldn't let him, and he was hanging on to whatever it was that was not healthy for him or this relationship they were starting.

"Can I come with you?" she asked, placing her hands on his shoulders.

"To see Thelma?"

Callie nodded. "She's obviously very important, Noah. I'd like to be there for you."

"That's not a good idea," he told her.

"Why not?"

His hands slid around her waist. "Because she's confused. She won't know who you are."

"If she's got Alzheimer's, then she won't even remember I was there." Callie squeezed his shoulders and slid her hands up to frame his face. "I want to be there for you, Noah. You've done so much for me. Please, let me do this for you."

His lips softly slid over hers before he leaned back and smiled. "Can you go tomorrow?"

"I'd love to."

Noah's nerves kept him up most of the night.

Since it was Friday, he had taken half a day off after doing some minor in-office surgeries. Now he and Callie were traveling to the assisted-living facility. He only prayed Thelma didn't start rambling about the wedding.

"I should warn you that Thelma may flirt with me."

Callie laughed. "Then she's sharp if she's flirting with a hot guy."

Noah reached over, gripped her hand. "Just don't get too jealous."

Once they arrived at the facility, Noah led the way to Thelma's room. As usual, the door was closed and locked. Noah knocked and waited.

Soon the door eased open and he reached over, gripping Callie's hand. She squeezed back, silently supporting him.

When Thelma saw him, then looked beyond and saw Callie, her whole face lit up.

"Malinda! My Malinda!"

Thelma reached out, pulling Callie beyond Noah and into a full embrace.

A feeling of dread overwhelmed him. He hadn't even thought that Thelma would mistake Callie for Malinda. Yes, the two had the same dark red hair, but he'd spent so much time with Callie lately he'd forgotten the similarities.

This was a bad, bad idea and nothing good would come from these next few minutes. He prayed to God again that Thelma didn't mention the wedding.

"Come in, come in." Thelma eased back. "I'm so glad you two are here."

Noah followed the ladies into the sweltering room. Once

again, he turned the heat down...way down. Because with his nerves, he was already sweating.

"I can't believe my Malinda is finally here," she gushed. "You're such a beautiful sight, my dear."

Callie glanced to Noah as if silently asking him to intervene.

"Thelma," he began. "This—"

"Is such a surprise." Thelma reached out for Callie's hand and squeezed. "I've been waiting for you to come." Thelma's eyes narrowed on Callie's face. "Darling, what happened?"

Callie's eyes sought Noah's again and he stepped forward. "She was in an accident, but she's fine. Just a cut."

Yeah, more lying to keep an old woman happy and worry-free.

"Oh, are you all right?" Thelma asked, searching Callie's face.

Callie offered a smile. "I'm fine. How are you doing?"

Thelma laughed. "I'm old. That's about it. I've been waiting for you to come. I can't wait to hear how the wedding is coming. Noah has told me very little. I want to hear more details from the bride-to-be."

"Oh, we're not engaged," Callie said. "We—"

Noah rested a hand on Callie's shoulder in the silent gesture for her to stop talking.

"Thelma loves to talk weddings, but I'd rather discuss how you're feeling today," he said, turning to Thelma. He had to change the subject.

Thelma waved a hand in the air. "I'm fine. I already told you. I'd much rather discuss the wedding of my beautiful granddaughter." Thelma pushed out of her recliner. "Hold on just a moment. I have something for you."

Callie turned to Noah and whispered, "Who does she think I am?"

Swallowing, Noah replied, "Her granddaughter."

"Were you engaged to this person?" she whispered between gritted teeth.

Noah could only nod. He was a coward. He was a jerk. Was he going to regret bringing her here, finally opening up to her in his own way?

Perhaps subconsciously he'd brought her here as a way to tell her. Callie deserved to know, and there was no easy way to break the news about his past.

"Here we are," Thelma stated as she came back with a photo. "I've had this here for a long time and I love looking at it, but I think maybe you could put it in your new home together."

Noah barely caught a glimpse of the photo as it passed from Thelma's hand to Callie's. And with that simple exchange, he knew any hope he'd had of not sharing the full truth with Callie was gone.

Callie looked down at the photo and nearly choked on instant tears that filled her. Noah had not only been engaged, but he'd been engaged to a woman who looked very similar to her.

Noah's arm was wrapped around the shoulders of this Malinda person and they were both smiling into the camera with their heads tilted toward each other. Callie wanted to tear it up, throw the confetti pieces into the air and run like hell out this door.

But because Thelma was looking at her with such hope and admiration, Callie smiled. "Thank you. This is wonderful."

"I'm giving this to you and hopefully you can give me another photo of the two of you, but this time I'd like one from the wedding."

Callie nodded. "Um, I'm not feeling so well."

Noah tried to put an arm over her shoulder, but Callie stepped aside. She didn't want him to touch her.

"Oh, darling," Thelma said with a frown. "Are you all right?"

"I'm just tired, I think. Would you mind if we discussed the wedding another time?"

"Of course." Thelma looked to Noah. "Get her home and take care of her."

"I intend to," Noah told her. "It was good to see you."

"Please, come back soon," Thelma said with a smile. "I miss seeing you both together. It just warms my heart."

Callie accepted the hug from the frail woman and managed not to burst into tears at the innocent endearment.

When they got back in the car, Callie didn't even know where to begin. The hurt was so deep, so all-consuming, she feared she'd break into a million pieces before she learned the full extent of his lies.

"You were engaged to her granddaughter?" Callie asked.

Noah sighed. He didn't start the car, didn't even turn to look at her...which should've told her the amount of guilt he carried.

"Yes."

She closed her eyes. "And you didn't think to mention that to me? Or the fact we have similar features?"

"Honestly—"

Callie laughed and glared at him. "Yes, Noah. Let's try for honesty."

Now he did turn to face her and Callie had to steel herself against the pain in his eyes.

"I didn't think you needed to know," he told her. "I didn't want my past to play a part in my present."

"Or your future?" Callie mocked. "Or did you not see me in your future, Noah? Did you think when I was healed I would just go back to my apartment, forget how good we were together and you could go on your way, too? Because I for one had envisioned more for us than just a few intimate moments. You met my family. You acted as if what we had was so much more. Was it all a lie? A way to pass the time until you got over your fiancée?"

"I never acted with you, Callie. And I never told you this was long-term."

That knife he'd stabbed her with slowly turned. "You never told me any different," she whispered through tears. "And your actions sure as hell told me what you were afraid to admit was in your heart. Apparently, you're still a coward."

But she would not cry. She'd hold on to this last bit of dignity she had.

"What happened to Malinda?" Callie asked, almost not wanting to hear the answer.

Noah's eyes hardened as he held her gaze. "She died of a drug overdose a year ago."

Of all the things she'd imagined him saying, that hadn't even made it on her list.

"She wanted to be an actress," he went on. "She wanted that big life she'd always dreamed of, and before I knew what was happening, she was hooked on drugs. Painkillers. I tried to get her help. She even went to rehab twice, but checked herself out both times."

Callie listened, knowing this confession was costing him, but right now they were both bleeding out for the other to see.

"I should've seen the signs earlier, should have done more. But in the end, I failed her."

Callie's heart broke for the man, the doctor who thought he should save everybody. But her heart also broke for herself at the realization of what he was *not* saying.

"So, was I the charity replacement?" she asked. "You couldn't save her so you thought you'd save me?"

Noah's gaze darted away, then came back. "I didn't see it that way, but probably in the beginning, yes. I didn't want to fail someone I cared about."

"Care about?" she cried. "You didn't care about me, Noah.

You cared about redeeming your flawed image of yourself. You cared about that damn ego and didn't once think about how this would hurt me, humiliate me. Did you think we'd just be intimate and I wouldn't fall for you? That I wouldn't start thinking long-term thoughts about us?"

She'd come this far, might as well rip the rest of the Band-Aid off.

"Did you think I wouldn't love you?" she whispered, no longer caring that tears had slid down her cheeks. She held his gaze, wanting him to see how he'd damaged her even more.

"I wish you'd never offered to help." Callie swiped at her unscarred cheek. "I would've much rather been on my own than know I was a fill-in for someone else."

He started to reach for her, but she shrank back against the door. "Don't even think of touching me."

Noah dropped his hand and nodded. "I didn't mean to hurt you, Callie. You've come to mean more to me than I wanted."

"If that were true, you wouldn't have used me as a replacement or tried to hide your past." She refused to listen to another lie or another excuse. "Take me home. And by *home,* I mean my apartment. You can bring my other things later and leave them on the stoop. I don't want to see you again, Noah."

"Callie, you can't mean that."

Her eyes slitted. "Oh, I mean it. And consider this my notice for the office. Effective immediately."

Sixteen

Noah moved through Callie's room. Her bed was rumpled where she'd slept, his shirts she'd worn were folded and lying on the trunk at the end of the bed. Her sandals were strewn around the room, and the second he stepped in here, he was enveloped by her sweet, floral aroma.

Noah gripped the edge of the dresser and closed his eyes. He'd majorly botched up everything he ever had with Callie. By protecting his heart, he'd completely crushed hers. What kind of man did that to an already vulnerable woman?

He glanced into the adjoining bath, his eyes instantly falling onto the tub where he'd helped her with her hair that first day. It was only six weeks ago, but so much had happened since then.

Aside from her quick healing, she'd opened up emotionally, she'd fought to not let her accident ruin her, he'd met her family and instantly felt a connection to them when they welcomed him into their home.

But the main thing that had happened was his heart had been taken over. Noah had sworn when Malinda died that no one would ever fill that void…and no one could. But he realized now that Callie found a new place in his heart to reside and she wasn't replacing Malinda at all. What he found with Callie was new, fresh and so real he didn't know why he hadn't seen it until that hurt, anger and despair flooded her eyes along with tears.

It was those tears that nearly killed him. He was the cause of those tears. He did this to her and he would have to be the one to fix it.

As a surgeon, he knew all too well that fixing things wasn't always simple or easy. But it was worth the time and effort.

And Callie Matthews was worth everything he had in him to give. He wasn't letting her go that easily.

Noah pulled his cell from his pocket and called his Realtor. This was just the first step in getting her back. For good.

Callie went right to work on her computer trying to find another job. At this point, she knew she couldn't be picky.

Noah had dropped her off that morning and here it was near dinnertime and he still hadn't brought her stuff. If he thought she'd be coming back, he was a total moron.

She'd cried in the shower until the water ran cold, then pulled on a blousy, sheer yellow top over a white tank and denim shorts. At least she could look cheerful even if she wasn't feeling it.

Callie had been on her laptop the past few hours because searching for work was productive and at least keeping her mind focused on something other than the fact that another fantasy, another dream had just been taken away by fate.

Callie refused to believe coming to L.A. was a mistake. She did love the town, and after going home, she knew for sure that being in the city suited her.

There were several tutoring jobs that she could start immediately and that would be good money until she could figure out what else she needed to do. She wasn't giving up on acting. Even though Noah had lied to her, Callie firmly believed what Max had told her about Anthony looking at her twice and she knew a makeup artist could work with her face.

She refused to let fate take control of her life. She'd let herself grow dependent on Noah by living with him, falling in love with him and focusing more on him than on her questionable career. And now she had to refocus on her original goal—acting.

But since she'd quit her job, she needed immediate funds that would keep a roof over her head, not to mention pay for the expense of the microdermabrasion. Perhaps she could take out a loan.

Someone knocked on her door and Callie froze. If that was Noah, he could just drop the stuff off and be on his way.

"I need to talk to you, Callie."

She closed her eyes and sighed. Might as well get this over with because her neighbors didn't deserve the bellowing.

Crossing the room, she jerked open the door. "What?"

His eyes raked over her body and she refused to allow the tingle to creep through and spear her heart anymore.

"Where's my stuff?" she asked, noting he held nothing and there was no luggage on the stoop.

"I want to take you somewhere," he told her.

She folded her arms over her chest, as if that would keep more hurt from seeping in. "You've got to be kidding me!"

"Just one hour, Callie. That's all I'm asking for, and at the end of that hour if you don't want to see me again, I'll walk away."

It was so tempting to slam the door in his face, but she couldn't do it. As much as she hated liars and deceivers, she wanted to know what he had in store for her.

"One hour," she told him. "No more."

His shoulders relaxed as he blew out a breath. "Thank you."

She grabbed her keys and her purse by the door and locked it behind her. By the time she was seated in his car, she wondered if she'd made a mistake. Now that she was in his presence, would she crumble and believe every word he said? She didn't want to be that woman who believed liars and found excuses to take them back.

"You look beautiful," he told her as he pulled out of her apartment complex.

"Don't. I don't need the pretty words."

"That time we went to celebrate your role, and you were standing there holding those yellow tickets, I thought of you as the color yellow," he went on as if she hadn't said anything. "I know it sounds stupid, but you're always so vibrant, so alive, and that smile you had on your face as you held that insane amount of tickets, I just thought if Callie were any color, it would be yellow."

She glanced down to her yellow top and closed her eyes. "What do you want from me, Noah?"

"A fresh start?"

Callie glanced across the spacious SUV and stared at him. "What?"

"I called my real-estate agent and accepted that last offer on my house. I'm moving back into my old house."

Her heart clenched as she fisted her hands in her lap to keep from reaching for him. "That's great."

"And I have a proposition for you, but you can take time to think about it."

Intrigued, and angry at her crumbling defenses, she asked, "What is it?"

He spared her a glance as he came to a red light. "I want

you to still model for me. I've made a decision on the new office I'm opening."

Reaching across, he took her hand and squeezed it. "I'm going to make it a surgical center for victims who have been scarred or burned."

Callie jerked her hand back, bringing it to her mouth in an attempt to hide her quivering chin. "Noah…"

He pulled ahead when the light changed and then turned into the pizza place where they'd "celebrated" weeks ago. Once the car was in Park, he faced her, taking both of her hands now.

"You've taught me so much, Callie. You can't know how you've opened my eyes to what's important." His eyes filled with unshed tears. "After meeting your family, learning even more about you and knowing how hard you've fought for what you want, I know that you are the woman I want in my life. I want your drive, your determination…your love."

Callie shook her head. "You don't mean that. You just see me as another woman who left you."

"You and Malinda may have similar appearances, but that's where the similarities stop. You have my heart, Callie, in a way I don't think she ever did. Yes, I'll always have a piece of me that loves her, but what I feel for you is so big, so beyond anything I've ever known. I can't give you up and I won't let you give up on us. Not when we're so close to perfection."

Callie glanced to the restaurant, saw all the kids inside playing games, getting tickets and running around with smiles.

She wanted to believe every word he said. She firmly believed that if he didn't truly love her, he wouldn't have acted so fast after she left. He wouldn't have sold his house, wouldn't have shown up at her door ready to fight for what they had.

She glanced back to him. "What are we doing here, Noah?"

His smile widened. "Celebrating."

"What are we celebrating?"

He reached behind her seat and pulled out the ugly monkey she'd won weeks ago. "It's not a ring, but I'm hoping you'll celebrate spending our lives together. Forever."

Callie looked at the pathetic stuffed animal and smiled through tears. "God, that was so romantic and silly at the same time." She laughed.

"What do you say we go in and win more ridiculous stuff to put in our house?"

She threw her arms around his neck and held tight. "I can't think of anything else I'd rather do."

Noah eased back, framed her face and kissed her lips. "I love you, Callie Matthews."

She saw the truth in his watery eyes. "I love you, too."

* * * * *

COMING NEXT MONTH from Harlequin Desire®
AVAILABLE JULY 1, 2013

#2239 ZANE
The Westmorelands
Brenda Jackson
No woman walks away from Zane Westmoreland! But when Channing Hastings does just that, the rancher vows to prove to her that there is no man for her but him.

#2240 RUMOR HAS IT
Texas Cattleman's Club: The Missing Mogul
Maureen Child
Hurtful gossip once tore Sheriff Nathan Battle and Amanda Altman apart. But when Amanda comes home, will an unexpected pregnancy drive a new wedge between them or finally heal old wounds?

#2241 THE SANTANA HEIR
Billionaires and Babies
Elizabeth Lane
Grace wants to adopt her late sister's son. Peruvian bachelor Emilio wants his brother's heir...and Grace in his bed. Can this bargaining-chip baby make them a *real* family?

#2242 A BABY BETWEEN FRIENDS
The Good, the Bad and the Texan
Kathie DeNosky
Wary of men but wanting a baby, Summer asks her best friend, rancher and bullfighter Ryder, to help her conceive. But can he share his bed with her without also sharing his heart?

#2243 TEMPTATION ON HIS TERMS
The Hunter Pact
Robyn Grady
Movie producer Dex Hunter needs a nanny, and Shelby Scott is perfect for the role. But when the script switches to romance, Shelby balks at the Hollywood happy ending, at least at first....

#2244 ONE NIGHT WITH THE SHEIKH
Kristi Gold
Recently widowed King Mehdi turns to former flame Maysa Barad for solace. But as forbidden desire resurfaces, betrayal and secrets threaten to destroy their relationship once and for all.

HDCNM0613

REQUEST YOUR FREE BOOKS!
2 FREE NOVELS PLUS 2 FREE GIFTS!

H HARLEQUIN®

Desire

ALWAYS POWERFUL, PASSIONATE AND PROVOCATIVE

YES! Please send me 2 FREE Harlequin Desire® novels and my 2 FREE gifts (gifts are worth about $10). After receiving them, if I don't wish to receive any more books, I can return the shipping statement marked "cancel." If I don't cancel, I will receive 6 brand-new novels every month and be billed just $4.55 per book in the U.S. or $4.99 per book in Canada. That's a savings of at least 13% off the cover price! It's quite a bargain! Shipping and handling is just 50¢ per book in the U.S. and 75¢ per book in Canada.* I understand that accepting the 2 free books and gifts places me under no obligation to buy anything. I can always return a shipment and cancel at any time. Even if I never buy another book, the two free books and gifts are mine to keep forever.

225/326 HDN F4ZC

Name _____ (PLEASE PRINT)

Address _____ Apt. #

City _____ State/Prov. _____ Zip/Postal Code

Signature (if under 18, a parent or guardian must sign)

Mail to the **Harlequin® Reader Service:**

IN U.S.A.: P.O. Box 1867, Buffalo, NY 14240-1867
IN CANADA: P.O. Box 609, Fort Erie, Ontario L2A 5X3

Want to try two free books from another line?
Call 1-800-873-8635 or visit www.ReaderService.com.

* Terms and prices subject to change without notice. Prices do not include applicable taxes. Sales tax applicable in N.Y. Canadian residents will be charged applicable taxes. Offer not valid in Quebec. This offer is limited to one order per household. Not valid for current subscribers to Harlequin Desire books. All orders subject to credit approval. Credit or debit balances in a customer's account(s) may be offset by any other outstanding balance owed by or to the customer. Please allow 4 to 6 weeks for delivery. Offer available while quantities last.

Your Privacy—The Harlequin® Reader Service is committed to protecting your privacy. Our Privacy Policy is available online at www.ReaderService.com or upon request from the Harlequin Reader Service.

We make a portion of our mailing list available to reputable third parties that offer products we believe may interest you. If you prefer that we not exchange your name with third parties, or if you wish to clarify or modify your communication preferences, please visit us at www.ReaderService.com/consumerschoice or write to us at Harlequin Reader Service Preference Service, P.O. Box 9062, Buffalo, NY 14269. Include your complete name and address.

HD13R

SPECIAL EXCERPT FROM

HARLEQUIN®

Desire

USA TODAY *bestselling author*

Kathie DeNosky presents

A BABY BETWEEN FRIENDS, *part of the series*

THE GOOD, THE BAD AND THE TEXAN.

Available July 2013 from Harlequin® Desire®!

They fell into a comfortable silence while Ryder drove through the star-studded Texas night.

Her best friend was the real deal—honest, intelligent, easygoing and loyal to a fault. And it was only recently that she'd allowed herself to notice how incredibly good-looking he was. That was one reason she'd purposely waited until they were alone in his truck where it was dark so she wouldn't have to meet his gaze.

The time had come to start the conversation that would either help her dream come true—or send her in search of someone else to assist her.

"I've been doing a lot of thinking lately…" she began. "I miss being part of a family."

"I know, darlin'." He reached across the console to cover her hand with his. "But one day you'll find someone and settle down, and then you'll not only be part of his family, you can start one of your own."

"That's not going to happen," she said, shaking her head. "I have absolutely no interest in getting married. These days it's quite common for a woman to choose single motherhood."

"Well, there are a lot of kids who need a good home," he concurred, his tone filled with understanding.

"I'm not talking about adopting," Summer said, "at least not yet. I'd like to experience all aspects of motherhood, if I can, and that includes being pregnant."

"The last I heard, being pregnant is kind of difficult without the benefit of a man being involved," he said with a wry smile.

"Yes, to a certain degree, a man would need to be involved."

"Oh, so you're going to visit a sperm bank?" He didn't sound judgmental and she took that as a positive sign.

"No." She shook her head. "I'd rather know my baby's father."

Ryder looked confused. "Then how do you figure on making this happen if you're unwilling to wait until you meet someone and you don't want to visit a sperm bank?"

Her pulse sped up. "I have a donor in mind."

"Well, I guess if the guy's agreeable that would work," he said thoughtfully. "Anybody I know?"

"Yes." She paused for a moment to shore up her courage. Then, before she lost her nerve, she blurted out, "I want you to be the father of my baby, Ryder."

Will Ryder say yes?

Find out in Kathie DeNosky's new novel

A BABY BETWEEN FRIENDS

Available July 2013 from Harlequin® Desire®!

HARLEQUIN Desire

ALWAYS POWERFUL, PASSIONATE AND PROVOCATIVE.

THE SANTANA HEIR

by Elizabeth Lane

Grace wants to adopt her late sister's son. Peruvian bachelor Emilio wants his brother's heir…and he wants Grace in his bed. Can this bargaining-chip baby make them a *real* family?

Look for the latest book in the scandalous *Billionaires and Babies* miniseries next month!

Available wherever books and ebooks are sold.

HD73254